DREAMWORKS

PUSS IN BOOTS

THE LAST WISH

JUNIOR NOVEL

D0062400

DreamWorks *Puss In Boots: The Last Wish* © 2022 DreamWorks
Animation LLC. All Rights Reserved. Written by Cala Spinner.
Scrapbook by Hannah Dussold. Designed by Jessica Meltzer Rodriguez.
All rights reserved. Printed in China. No part of this book may be used or
reproduced in any manner whatsoever without written permission except
in the case of reprints in the context of reviews.

Andrews McMeel Publishing
a division of Andrews McMeel Universal
1130 Walnut Street, Kansas City, Missouri 64106

www.andrewsmcmeel.com

22 23 24 25 26 27 28 RLP 10 9 8 7 6 5 4 3 2 1

ISBN: 978-1-5248-7755-2

Made by:
Shenzhen Reliance Printing Co., Ltd
25 Longshan Industrial Zone, Nanling
Longgang District, Shenzhen 518114, China

1st Printing—April 7th, 2022

ATTENTION: SCHOOLS AND BUSINESSES

Andrews McMeel books are available at quantity discounts with
bulk purchase for educational, business, or sales promotional use.
For information, please e-mail the Andrews McMeel Publishing
Special Sales Department: specialsales@amuniversal.com

DREAMWORKS

PUSS IN BOOTS
THE LAST WISH

JUNIOR NOVEL

Andrews McMeel
PUBLISHING®

TABLE OF CONTENTS

PROLOGUE

Once upon a time, a wishing star fell from the sky and landed in a forest.

On impact, the star scorched the trees, and the forest became known as the Dark Forest. From then on, no one went inside—and no one came out.

However, the wishing star lay hidden deep in the Dark Forest's center. It promised to grant one wish—and only one—to whoever was lucky enough to find it.

Of course, this is a fairy tale. And real life is way different from fairy tales. Right?

CHAPTER 1

The cat Puss in Boots needed no introduction. But in case you forgot, he was a legend who went by many names: Diablo Gato. The Furry Lover. El Chupacabra. Friskie Two-Times. The Ginger Hitman. And of course, Puss.

Such an accomplished cat needed well-deserved praise. But even more than praise, he needed a party! Puss was preparing for the Fiesta del Puss in a cliffside mansion in Del Mar.* And like any party of his, it would be great.

---

*In case you're wondering, "How did Puss get a cliffside mansion in Del Mar?" do not fret—all will be revealed soon! Just put your trust in Puss.

Puss stood outside the ballroom, preparing himself for the party. Though already equipped with his cavalier hat and trusty sword, he needed to practice all his moves to bedazzle the socks—and boots—off of everyone.

"Tcha tcha oo, cha," Puss said, mimicking a fencing lunge. His paws moved swiftly and accurately. "Oh yeah, I'm good," Puss reminded himself happily. He was ready for the fiesta!

Puss waltzed into the banquet hall to meet his guests. He shimmied through the throngs of attendees, admiring all the partygoers as they danced to the live band.

"Welcome to my fiesta!" Puss said. The partygoers, all decked out in strange and fine rags, held up their merriment to the sky.

"Make yourselves at home," continued Puss. "Eat."

He picked up a kabob from the food spread and waved it around, pretending it was a sword. The crowd went wild.

"And drink!"

Puss leapt and flipped onto nearby barrels. With one clean swipe of his sword, he uncorked three barrels of leche and watched as the drink cascaded downward.

The partygoers cheered. They filled their glasses to the brim with leche and sang Puss's praises as he made his way through the crowd.

And we do mean *through* the crowd. Puss traipsed over

4

a few outstretched palms, a hook, a hoof, and a child's face.

"Papa! He stepped on my face!" the child cried.

"And we will *never* wash it again!" the child's father called back, making sure Puss knew their loyalty to him remained unwavering.

Puss made his way onto a high balcony railing. The crowd couldn't stop clapping and looking upon him with wonder. A spotlight found Puss, and he took this opportunity to throw handfuls of gold into the audience below.

"People of Cordova!" cried Puss.

"It's Del Mar!" one partygoer interjected.

"People of Del Mar! Accept this golden gift from . . . Puss in Boots!" Puss cheered, while chucking the gold out into his sea of adoring fans.

"Play a song!" one fan requested.

Puss smiled, feigning modesty. "No, no, no. I couldn't."

"Sing for us!" another partygoer chimed.

Even the cows moo'ed in agreement. *Moooooo.* (That translates to, "Sing for us, Puss," in *Moo.*)

"I couldn't possibly . . ." Puss trailed off.

Of course, this was his plan all along. He raised a paw. Magically, his guitar flew right into it.

Puss began strumming the guitar. He played some gnarly flamenco solos, stomping in rhythm as the house band joined in. It was a fiesta for the record books!

"Who is your favorite fearless hero?" Puss sang. "Who is brave and ready for trouble?"

The crowd joined in.

"You are. You are!" they cheered.

Puss threw balls of yarn into the crowd like beach balls.

"Who is so unbelievably humble?"

"You are. You are!" the crowd continued.

Puss was riding the party wave. He stage-dived into the crowd, through the partygoers, and up to the barrels of leche.

"Who is the cat who rolls the dice?" Puss called. "And gambles with his life?"

"You are!" the crowd sung.

"Who's never been touched by a blade?" Puss added as an after-thought.

"You are! You are!"

"Who is your favorite fearless hero?" he called out, this time dancing with a chicken.

Puss continued playing guitar and the crowd continued cheering. He swung around the banquet hall on curtains. Until . . .

CREEEEAK! The mansion door opened. Two high-heeled boots (very stuffy, in Puss's opinion, for boots) entered with luggage. The band stopped playing and Puss stopped singing.

It was the governor! He was a pompous bureaucrat in a powdered wig, just now returning from vacation. And in case you were wondering how Puss bought a mansion . . . he hadn't. (See? The answer, as promised!) The mansion belonged to the governor. And the governor didn't know about Fiesta del Puss.

The governor dropped his suitcases in disbelief.

"My clothes!" he gasped angrily, as it became clear the peasants had raided his wardrobe and were parading around in his finest threads.

"My wig!" the governor cried. It was sitting atop the head of an Andalusian horse.

"My portrait!" the governor bellowed. His lordly portrait had been painted over so that it now had the head of Puss in Boots.

And the governor, now understanding who was at the helm of such a heist, locked eyes with Puss, who was suspended above on one of the governor's curtains.

"The outlaw, Puss in Boots!" he wailed.

Puss descended slowly. With a smirk, he turned to the governor on the rail of the balcony, still holding his guitar.

"Welcome! Mi casa es su casa," Puss called.

The governor was furious. "No, su casa es MI casa!" he said. "Arrest these filthy peasants and bring me the head of Puss in Boots!"

Armed guards ran in with their swords drawn. Puss, sensing the danger, dropped his guitar and drew his sword, ready for battle.

But first things first.

Puss turned to the band.

"Hey! This is a party! Where is the music?"

Jolting to a start, the band continued their song.

He's the blade of justice. Stands up against evil. Fighting for the people. And he's very good looking. Who is your favorite fearless hero? Puss in Boots.

Puss fought his way through the governor's guards, dispatching them easily and taking them down like large bowling pins. At last, he faced the governor.

The governor drew his sword and made some fancy thrusts and swipes at the air. However, he was no match for Puss. Puss parkoured off the toppled hors d'oeuvres table and leapt onto his ice sculpture. He skated off the ice and slid toward the governor, who aimed at Puss, but only managed to cut off the sculpture's head.

Puss took a moment to pose with the decapitated ice.

"Puss in Boots has never been touched by a blade!" Puss called. His eyes squared on the governor. "But you?"

As if on cue, the governor's wig split, followed by his collar. The letter "P" cut into his chest, and then his pants fell around his ankles! Puss had gotten him in a sneak attack.

The governor stood in the banquet hall in just his undies. Naturally, the crowd laughed and pointed at him.

"Skin that cat!" the governor cried out in fury.

But Puss had a plan. He struck a match and revealed that his final move. Fireworks!

"Governor," Puss said. "Lighten up."

He touched the match to a fuse. *FLASH!*

Meanwhile, outside, the sky above the governor's mansion exploded with fireworks. They were louder than thunder and more beautiful than anything the people of Del Mar had ever seen. The sound boomed and ricocheted off the mountaintops . . .

Which awakened a mountain giant in the outskirts of Del Mar and made him stir. (Of course, Puss doesn't know that yet. So don't tell Puss, pretty please.) The mountain giant had antlers and one glowing, searchlight eye. An eyepatch covered the other eye.

The mountain giant looked at the governor's mansion and headed toward it.

Back at the mansion, the governor's guards were back. They dog-piled Puss on the floor. All the crowd could see was a heap of tangled limbs and armor. After a moment, one guard stuck his hand out from the top of the pile, seemingly victorious.

Alas, there was a rustle at a nearby table. It was Puss! He was standing and drinking some leche, no less.

"Silly guards. Dog piles don't work on cats," Puss said.

But his excitement was short lived when . . . a pair of *mountain giant hands ripped off the roof!*

CHAPTER 2

The mountain giant's hands ripped right through the governor's cliffside mansion and tore its roof off. From the banquet hall, the partygoers could see the mountain giant peering in, one eye aglow.

"Holy frijoles!" Puss called out.

"You awoke the Sleeping Giant of Del Mar!" shrieked someone in the crowd.

Angry, the giant collected screaming captives in his giant wooden fanny-pack. He reached in and scooped up a handful of guards with one simple swipe.

Puss leapt into action, ready to save his partygoers. He ran over the tables and across the mansion, all the while keeping his stride with the giant.

As people ran for cover, the giant tore off another portion of the roof. The giant reached in to grab a boy riding a cow.

"Wee! I'm flying!" the boy said.

"No, you are not flying," Puss called back. (Flying is NOT when a mountain giant picks you up, fun fact.) Then, in his best hero voice, Puss bellowed, "I will save you!"

But before Puss could save the boy riding his cow, the governor got snatched up, too.

"Save me, too!" the governor bellowed.

Puss shrugged and said, "If it's convenient."

Then, without skipping a beat, the band's guitarist launched Puss up to the giant by pulling back the strings on his guitar like a bow. Puss rocketed skyward and soared through the air, ready for action with his sword drawn.

Puss knew that he had to strike. *FFFT!* He entered the mountain giant's range and stuck his sword right under the giant's fingernail. The giant yelled in horror. The crowd did, too.

"The Spanish Splinter!" Puss bellowed.

For its next move, the mountain giant hurled Puss through the village.

While midair, Puss grabbed the sign off the local pub as he flew past, using it as a shield. The momentum from the giant's throw sent him crashing through tenant buildings, multiple apartments, and, finally, a kitchen where a man sat enjoying a glass of leche.

Puss gently took his cup.

"Gracias," he said.

He chugged the leche. *Meow.* Puss then slammed the empty glass back on the table. Any damage he had sustained during the giant attack was now cured. He was fully revived! Puss leapt back into the thick of the fight.

"Fear me, if you dare!" Puss called.

Puss jumped out onto the rooftops, running at full speed. He dashed toward the bell tower at the center of town. The mountain giant may have had a wounded finger, but he could still fight. The giant ripped the bell right out of the tower and swung it around like a wrecking ball.

Puss leapt from roof to roof, avoiding the bell. The bell clanged and chimed as it smashed through the village. Finally, the bell smashed right beside Puss in a narrow miss. Puss grabbed hold of it right as the mountain giant whipped it backup unto the air. He then flung himself toward the giant, spinning like a throwing star until Puss landed on the giant's fanny pack.

Puss expertly cut the satchel's strap, sending the captives onto the ground and into freedom. They cheered and ran. The boy and his cow—as well as the other less important victims, like the governor—were safe.

Making jaw-dropping jumps, spinning through the air, and finally landing with his sword planted in the giant's back, Puss was on the final attack. The giant screamed as Puss wedged himself into the giant's ear.

"Hey giant, pray for mercy," Puss yelled in his final battle cry. "From Puss in Boots." He grabbed the giant's eyepatch, swung on it, and slid over to the giant's good eye. Out of shock and desperation, the giant swung the bell he was still holding out of control. Its rope caught around the giant's antlers, cinching him into further defeat.

Then Puss delivered the winning blow—the bell slammed hard into the giant's face. *DONNNNGGGGGG!* The giant reeled back slowly like a falling tree.

Victorious, Puss hopped to safety in front of his adoring spectators. He used his sword to slow his speed, carving a giant "P"—his signature move—in the dirt.

"Lo mas fuerte, legenda vivente, ta-da!" Puss sang.

Puss stood before his fans, drinking in the praise. A chicken ran up to him with a bouquet of pink flowers in its beak.

"Gracias, Del Mar! You've been great! Get home safely. Good night!" Puss called out like he was the biggest rockstar ever. But he wasn't done just yet. It was encore time.

"I call this one 'The Legend Will Never Die,'" Puss said, always ready for more attention.

But then . . .

KA-DONG!!!

The loose church bell fell right on Puss, smashing him completely flat.

CHAPTER 3

"Puss? Puss? Puss in Boots?"

Puss opened his eyes slowly. At first, he didn't know where he was. There were no adoring fans, no fiesta, no band. Then his eyes zeroed in on all the strange things in the room. There were jars of brine, racks of malformed skulls, bone saws, and scalpels. Standing before him was an energetic oddball with a fancy hairdo who was expertly sharpening a barber's knife.

"Where—where am I?" Puss stuttered.

"Not to worry. You're in good hands. *My* hands," the oddball said. He lifted Puss's arms up. "I am the village doctor." He examined Puss with a new array of instruments, all rapid-fire. Stethoscope, scissors, tongue depressor, medicinal powder . . .

"I am also the village barber, veterinarian, dentist, and witch-finder," he added, blowing powder into Puss's face. "And in my professional opinion, you need a wash, a blow-out, and a little trim around the headquarters."

"Um," Puss squeaked out.

"That's my professional *barber* opinion. But!" The man turned away and outfitted himself with a new hat that was adorned with a candle. "Putting on my doctor's hat, I think we need to run a few tests." The oddball-slash-vet leaned in and pulled out a mallet.

"Alright, reflexes—"

BONK! He tapped the mallet on Puss's knee. Puss cat-slapped the vet's face ten times with his paws.

"Cat-like," the vet noted. "Temperature! Now lift your tail and relax." Said the vet, spinning Puss around. Before he could do anything Puss gasped and spun back around, grabbing the thermometer from the vets hands and placing it in the vet's shirt pocket.

"Trust me: I run hot. Yup," said Puss.

The vet continued with enthusiasm, "Then how about the latest in modern medical technology? Leeches! To draw out the evil humors."

Puss hissed at the vet, coming toward him with a screeching leech. "Suit yourself," replies the vet. "More for me." He dropped the leech down his shirt.

"Listen, doctor. Thanks for everything, you know, but I am feeling great," Puss said, now that he'd come to. He flexed his arms "Strong, like a bull! You know. Now . . . do you know a good place to get some gazpacho?"

"Please," the vet pleaded. "This is serious."

"What is it?" Puss asked.

"Puss in Boots, how do I say this . . .?" The vet removed the candle from his hat and put a hand on Puss's shoulder. "You died."

Puss was nonplussed.

"Relax! I am Puss in Boots. I laugh at death. Ha, ha, ha, ha! You see, I am a cat. I have *nine lives*."

The vet pulled down his glasses.

"And how many times have you died already?" he asked.

Puss shrugged. "I dunno, I never counted. I'm not really a 'math guy,' you know?"

The vet looked at him expectantly. Puss decided to humor him.

"Alright, doctor. Let's see. There was the running of the bulls in Pamplona, poker-playing dogs in Monaco, tall tower leap in Munich, the medieval gymnasium in France, cannon shot in Portugal, shellfish allergy at the restaurant, oven explosion on Drury Lane . . . and then there was the giant today!" Puss recalled. "So, what is that, like, four?"

"That makes eight, Puss," the vet said. "You are down to your last life. My prescription: no more adventures for you! You need to retire."

Retire? "Are you the village comedian as well?"

But the vet wasn't laughing.

"Puss. Is there any safe place you can go? Any special someone you can rely on in this moment of need?"

"I am Puss in Boots, loved by one and all," Puss replied.

"Anyone in particular?" the vet asked.

Puss squirmed, uncomfortable. Why would the doctor need to know about his past? All he needed to know was that he was the *legendary* Puss in Boots!

"I mean, uh, how could I possibly choose?" he said.

Taking note of this, the vet scribbled on a strip of paper and then handed it to him.

"This is the address of Mama Luna. She is a cat-fancier, always on the lookout for a new lap-cat. You will be safe there," the vet said.

Lap-cat?! The vet really *was* a comedian. Puss jumped down from the exam table and grabbed his sword.

"I am no lap-cat, doctor!" Puss hollered. "I am . . . Puss in Boots!" He sheathed his sword.

The vet sighed. "Not anymore. Barber's orders. I mean, doctor's orders. Remember, Puss. Death comes for us all."

Puss felt angry. He started to walk out, but the vet had one more trick up his sleeve. He pulled out a jar of cat treats and offered one to Puss, who reluctantly took it.

"You've really got to work on your bedside manner," Puss said in between angry munches. Before he stormed off for good, he decided to take the whole treat jar. After all, they were pretty good.

CHAPTER 4

Puss felt dejected. That night, he found himself at a late-night tavern, lapping small cups of heavy cream and contemplating his future.

"I am . . . Puss in Boots," Puss said, in between licks of leche. "I am no one's lap-cat. That doctor is a quack. He should stick to cutting hair."

"Last call, Señor Boots," the tavern server shouted.

"Another glass of cream. Make it your heaviest," Puss mumbled sadly. The server left to get it from the backroom.

A draft blew through the tavern, blowing out all the candles. Puss caught his reflection and lifted his leche as a toast. "Hah! Retire . . . you are too good-looking to retire."

Then Puss heard whistling. It was tuneless, haunting, and . . . close. Through the reflection in the mirror, Puss realized he didn't see someone sitting on the stool next to him. He peeked over and saw it was a hooded wolf, who gave him a toothy smile and raised his own glass.

"Well, if it isn't Puss in Boots himself," the wolf said, chuckling. "In the flesh." He surveyed Puss's confused face in the reflection of his drink. "There's the famous hat. The feather. And of course, the *boots*. My compliments to your cobbler."

"Thanks, uh, good to meet you, too," Puss said. There was something about the wolf that made him feel nervous and uneasy.

"Hey. I never do this, but can I get your autograph? I've been following you for a long time," the wolf said. He pulled out a Puss in Boots "Wanted" poster and unrolled it, letting the "Wanted: Dead or Alive" message unfurl at top. Then he tapped the word "dead" and said, "Sign right there."

Okay, that made Puss feel VERY uneasy.

"Ha ha. Puss in Boots laughs in the face of death, *bounty hunter*!" Puss said.

"Everyone thinks they'll be the one to defeat me, but no one's escaped me yet," the wolf said.

Puss sighed. "Alright. Let's get it over with." With his signature gusto, Puss drew his sword. "Fear me, if you—"

CLANG! Puss's sword was swiped out of his paw and into a barrel. Without taking his eyes off the wolf, Puss ran backward to retrieve his sword.

"Okay, no more messing around. Hah!" Sword back in hand, Puss charged. But the wolf dodged Puss's attacks with ease.

"Slow. Sloppy. Sad," the wolf remarked.

The wolf pulled out two sickles with flashing blades. He and Puss battled in a furious exchange of steel-on-steel, blade versus sword. The wolf was right—he *was* strong.

"You're not living up to the legend, gato," the wolf said.

The wolf pinned Puss down and tossed him into a nearby chair. The wolf was preternaturally fast, his attacks relentless. He flipped a table over toward Puss, forcing him on his heels as they crossed blades. Then, in a defining uppercut, the wolf's sickle swung across, knocking off Puss's cavalier hat, and *cutting* Puss's brow! *CLING!* Puss's sword clattered to the ground.

Amidst all of this, Puss gasped. Something was wrong. *Something had changed.* Blood dripped down from the middle of his brow. He'd been . . . hurt?

"Ahhh. I just love the smell of fear," the wolf said. He

walked toward Puss, dragging his sickles menacingly across the stone floor. "What's the matter? Lives flashing before your eyes?"

Puss glanced at his sword. He didn't know what to do. His eyes darted from the sword to the wolf and back again. The wolf kicked the sword toward Puss and said, "Pick it up."

Puss looked down at his sword again, frozen with fear. "Pick. It. Up!" Puss heard the wolf growl. Now, the *legend* would have picked his sword up and bravely faced this strange, new adversary. But instead, Puss did the one thing he'd sworn would never befall him—he fled, leaving his sword behind.

"Corre corre, gatito," the wolf chuckled.

Puss escaped through the sewers and out of town. He ran through the forest all night until he finally arrived outside of a walled-off compound atop a hill. This wasn't where he wanted to go, but he was left with no choice. Puss looked at the card his vet gave him and confirmed this was the place: Mama Luna's compound.

As Puss entered the compound's front yard, he teared

up. Reaching the compound meant truly saying goodbye to the legend he once was.

"I am no longer worthy. I'm sorry," Puss said while clutching a rose. With only one life left, he was too afraid to continue on as he once did.

He removed his cat, cape, belt, and finally, his boots. Then he dug a grave into the ground as he buried his signature attire. The grave was in the shape of Puss's silhouette. He might have been the only one at the faux funeral, but he wasn't going to spare any dramatics.

"We are gathered here today to say goodbye to Puss in Boots," Puss said. "There are no words to express such a loss. Thank you."

Gaining some momentum, he then added, "But it would be a crime not to try. He was known across the land by many names. The Stabby Tabby! El Macho Gato! The Leche Whisperer. To some, an outlaw. To more, a hero. To all, a legend. I was right. Words were not enough."

Then Puss sang his song, all the while crying. He concluded the funeral by kicking back dirt onto the grave. He planted a branch in the shape of a "P" over it like a headstone. Then he walked away and onto the house's porch to start his new life.

CHAPTER 5

The compound was Mama Luna's place. Everything at Mama Luna's was cat-themed, from the weathervane spinning on the roof, to the chimes ringing in the breeze, to the porcelain cat mechanically waving its paw.

Puss sharply bent at the waist as he assumed the stance of an average, four-legged cat. Then he knocked at the door.

From the inside, a voice rang out.

"Now, I done told you health department people, there are no cats here!"

"Uh," Puss cleared his throat. "Meow?"

This was the magic word. The woman—Mama Luna— opened the door.

"Oh! You're not from the health department, are you? No, you're not," Mama Luna said. She picked Puss up and clutched him close to her chest. "We better get you inside because, baby, *they are always watching.*"

Mama Luna gently carried Puss into her parlor. It was teeming with stacked bags of kibble and kitty-litter sacks. Puss had never seen anything like it.

"I am Mama Luna. And this is my home. Now it's your home, too. Your *forever* home," she said, emphasizing the word "forever."

True to her word, Mama Luna *did* take care of Puss. She dunked him in water and gave him a sudsy bath. Then she dried him off with a towel and gave him a pair of mittens.

"I bet you've never even had a name," she remarked to Puss. "But you know what, I have thought of something perfect! I shall call you—Pickles!"

Mama Luna held up Puss, now with a leather collar that said "Pickles," to introduce him to the other cats.

"Brother cats! Sister kitties! Meet your new roommate." She set Puss down and stared at him. "Say hello to your new family!"

Puss watched as the crowd of cats stared at him.

"Meow?" Puss offered.

The cats hissed and covered their mouths, both shocked and offended.

"What, did I say something salty? It's actually my second language," Puss said.

Later that day, Puss needed to use the toilet, so he shimmied into Mama Luna's bathroom and stood on the rim of the toilet, per usual. But then—*SPRRRT!*—a spray bottle squirted him!

"Oh no, silly Pickles. This is a person potty. That's your potty," Mama Luna cooed, pointing to a litter box, which was currently being occupied by a cat named Checkers, followed by a horde of waiting cats.

Puss looked at it, feeling dismayed.

"So, this is where dignity goes to die," he said.

It was difficult for Puss to adjust to—er—*lap-cat* life. For mealtime, Mama Luna ripped open a bag of kibble with her teeth and set out the pellets for everyone to eat. Puss sniffled the kibble. Was it food? The other cats seemed to think so, but for Puss, absolutely not. Later, when he was sure that Mama Luna wasn't looking, he stood at the stove, ready to make himself a meal. But alas, Mama

Luna found him. She sprayed him with the testy bottle and said, "No cooking."

Relaxing wasn't much better. When Puss found a patch of sunlight to lay in, the horde of other cats surrounded him, wanting to lie in the sun, too. Puss gazed up toward the ceiling. He felt like a crowded sardine.

On day two at Mama Luna's, Puss decided to do something out of desperation. He *tried* some of the kibble. It was crunchy and disgusting, just as he expected. But it was food.

By day three, Puss was miserable and resigned to his fate. He waited for the litter box, just like the other cats. As the kibble was poured, Puss assimilated and ate it, just like the rest of the colony. His transformation into a fully bearded, scruffy house cat was complete. He was miserable, but alive.

While eating the kibble, Puss noticed a tail next to him wagging quite overzealously. Puss looked up, irritated. He brushed the tail out of his face.

Do you mind? I'm trying to eat here," Puss said. I mean, meow-whatever."

The tail-owner looked up, but it wasn't a cat at all. It was a *dog*. A tiny, teacup mutt in a filthy sweater, pretending to be a cat with broom bristles for whiskers and a feather duster for a tail!

"Sorry," the dog said. Then it sunk in. "Oh, oh, oh! You're a talking cat? *I'm* a talking cat! Let's talk!"

Puss sighed. "I'd rather eat," he said.

"Not a problem!" replied the dog. He took a mouthful of kibble and sputtered, "We can eat and talk at the same time!"

"No hablo Inglés," Puss muttered.

"Hablas Español? Yo también! De donde eres? Te gusta las siestas?"

"I don't speak Spanish either."

"Ha! You're funny," replied the dog.

Puss sighed again. "Okay, good talk." He motioned to walk away, but the dog was too quick. He parted Puss's beard to find the "Pickles" tag.

"Oh, hang on! Pickles? Is that your name? Me, I don't have a name. Or a home . . . so I'm no expert. But you don't look like a Pickles."

Puss knew that the dog must have been adoptable and homeless for some time, but he didn't care. "Well, *you* don't look like a cat," Puss pointed out.

This made the dog look anxious. "Okay, okay, full disclosure—I'm not a cat. I'm a dog. I live under the porch. It can get a little lonely down there. It's mostly controlled by the rats and the centipedes, but I have my own little corner."

"Congratulations," Puss said.

"I just come up here for the food and the friends." As the dog said that, the cats hissed at him. "Okay, so, mostly the food. Please don't tell anyone. I need this!"

"I won't tell. I don't care," Puss replied.

"*So*, you'll keep my secret? A secret between *friends*?" the dog pleaded.

"Just a secret," said Puss.

"It's funny. Despite all this best-friend bonding, you're still a mystery to me, Pickles. What's your story?"

"My story?" Puss repeated. Of all the things that had happened, this angered him most. "My *story* is over!"

The dog considered how dark this was for a second. Then he came up with a solution to pivot from Puss's dramatics. "Wanna rub my belly?" He sat back on his haunches and slowly hiked up his sweater, revealing a pudgy puppy belly.

"Hard pass," Puss muttered.

The dog told Puss that he needed the practice. He aspired to be a therapy dog one day. "When people feel bad, they should rub my belly. It'll make them feel better!" Then, squaring his eyes on Puss, he repeated, "go ahead, rub my belly."

"No."

"C'mon. Rub it!"

"No. Not happening," Puss hissed.

"Rub it!"

"No. Let me be clear. I don't want to touch your belly. Okay?" Puss ran up a cat tower and laid down in the hammock. He'd already been humiliated enough.

"Okey doke. So, what do you want?" the dog asked.

Puss kicked off his bottom booties as he settled into the hammock. What *did* he want? He couldn't go back to being the legend he once was, but perhaps Puss couldn't resign himself to this fate as well as he thought he could. Was this really all that was left for him?

Finally, Puss said simply, "I want to be left alone."

The dog curled up at the base of the cat tower.

Back in Del Mar, the Three Bears Crime Family would prove an obstacle for Puss's plans. They had heard of the fight with the sleeping giant and came because they had business with the legendary feline.

The three bears—Mama Bear, Papa Bear, and Baby Bear—lumbered through the streets searching for Puss. Atop Mama Bear rode a blond-haired girl holding a big shepherd's staff: Goldilocks.

"You got the scent?" Goldilocks asked Mama Bear.

She was looking at the footprints of a chicken, but they seemed too small. And then she saw a massive footprint from the giant, but that seemed too big.

Finally, Goldilocks squared in on some of Puss's boot prints. She added it suspiciously.

"But these ones . . . these ones are just right."

Goldilocks and the three bears went to track that cat.

CHAPTER 6

Puss, sporting his new haggard beard, squatted in the litter box, completing his business.

"Whatcha doin'?" the dog asked him.

"Ugh. You're back," Puss demurred.

"Oh, I never left."

Puss was just about to quip back when he heard a creaking sound, which didn't make sense because Mama Luna lay asleep in her armchair and all the other cats lay napping around the house. Something heavy walked outside on the wooden planking at Mama Luna's. Puss noticed a shadow pass in the window. The doorknob jiggled. A big nose sniffed under the door . . .

For one of the few times in his many lives, Puss was scared. Was it the wolf? Had he found him?

BOOM! With seemingly little effort from outside, the front door opened and smashed into splinters. But it wasn't the wolf. (You thought it was the wolf, didn't you? So did Puss.)

It was Papa Bear and Baby Bear.

The following scene was quite disastrous. Yowling cats raced up the curtains and the bookshelves. Puss took cover beneath a side table, peering fearfully from the shadows. The dog zipped in next to him.

As the dust cleared, Goldilocks entered the front door and motioned toward Mama Luna visibly shaken after her abrupt awakening. "Hello, missus," Goldilocks said, holding up Puss's wanted poster. "We're looking for a cat. This cat. We've got an offer for him."

An offer? For Puss? What could they possibly have to offer him?

"What's a Puss in Boots?" Dog asked. (What? Did you expect us to just keep calling him "the dog" all the time?)

"Seriously?" Puss quipped.

But Mama Luna stood her ground. "Get your paws off me! I told you health department people, there are no cats here."

Goldilocks exchanged a glance with Paper Bear.

"Make her talk," she commanded.

Papa Bear stood on his hind legs, getting nose-to-nose with Mama Luna until he turned into a proper gentlebear.

"Excuse me, my darling, we're looking for the legendary Puss in Boots. Have you perhaps seen him?"

Mama Luna grabbed a broom next to her and broke it over Papa Bear's head. "Too soft," Goldilocks remarked.

In response, Mama Bear tightened her hold, using a single long claw as a dagger against Mama Luna. This was too much for Mama Luna, who fainted and slid through Mama Bear's grip.

"Too hard! That was *not* just right," Goldilocks scolded. "Oi, Baby! Sniff him out."

"You don't tell me what to do. You're not my sister; you're a fugitive orphan," said Baby Bear. But Papa Bear slapped him on the back of his head. (This action isn't exactly recommended for human parents, but Baby and Papa were bears. Baby knew he had to obey.)

"She *is* your sister! Do as she says," said Papa Bear.

"Fine. But all I can smell is cat pee."

Mama Luna came to, running through the scene with an armful of cats.

"Everybody, get to the safe room! Just like we practiced!" she hollered. "Follow me, children!"

"Give her the piano treatment, Papa!" Mama Bear

called out. Papa Bear snatched Mama Luna from running off and stuffed her into the top of an upright piano.

"You think this is the first time I've been stuffed in a piano?" Mama Luna shouted from inside.

With Mama Luna momentarily out of the way again, Mama Bear created some ruckus by trying on some of Luna's hats. Meanwhile, Baby sniffed his way over to a closet and opened it, unleashing a pile of hissing kittens. Half the cats bolted through the house in terror. The other half scrambled up Baby and covered him.

"Arrgh!" Baby yelped. "There's cats everywhere! There's so many cats!" He smashed through a window and fell outside.

From his hiding place, Puss watched it all with Dog. They were such amateurs—nothing compared to the legendary Puss in Boots! He was quite amused.

Still on the hunt, Mama Bear grabbed, examined, and then presented Dog to Goldilocks.

"That's a dog in a cat costume," Goldilocks said.

"Oh yeah . . . tricky little bugger," Mama Bear replied, acknowledging her mistake. Then she yanked Puss out from his hiding spot. "How about this one," she said. "He's a ginger . . ."

Goldilocks held up the wanted poster again.

"Is that a joke? You think *this* scruffy, ancient bag of bones looks like a legend? This is definitely not—"

As Goldilocks was hollering, Baby Bear called from outside, "Puss in Boots! I found him! Dead and buried."

Goldilocks raced outside, followed by Mama and Papa Bear. Sure enough, they came upon the grave that Puss had made.

"Well, that's that then. What say we go and hibernate, eh?" Papa Bear suggested.

"No! We are *not* giving up. Jack's goons *finally* found the map, and it's getting delivered *tonight*. Without Puss, we'll never steal it! And without the map we'll never find the wishing star!" Goldilocks said. "That star has *one* wish to grant. Think of what it could mean for *us*."

Puss heard it all from his perch behind a bush.

The wishing star was real? It wasn't just a fairy tale? He could hardly believe it! This was the answer he'd been looking for! He could restore his nine lives—and become the legendary Puss in Boots once more! It would be a Fiesta del Puss for the *ages*.

"Well, I don't see why we needed to hire Puss in Boots in the first place," Baby Bear said.

"Because nobody steals from Big Jack Horner," Goldilocks replied.

Puss's eyes got as wide as saucers. Not *the* Jack Horner! Robbin' Big Jack Horner owned the pie factory and was known for his fascination with magical artifacts (and his tight security). But if the map was getting delivered tonight, there may be a chance to steal it before Jack locked it away forever. It was risky, but if the wishing star could get Puss his lives back—and his *life* back—he had to try.

He watched as Goldilocks and the three bears walked away, intent on their own plan. Then Puss threw off the mittens that Mama Luna had given him.

"Goodbye, Pickles!" he cheered.

Little did Puss know, Dog was right beside him—*again*.

"Oh no, Pickles. You're leaving?"

Puss pointed to the grave. "Perro! Start digging!" he commanded.

Dog got right to it, unearthing Puss's costume.

"Okay. But if this Puss in Boots is such a big deal, maybe we shouldn't be desecrating his grave."

Puss smiled, quickly dressing himself in his hat, boots, cape, and belt. "I don't think he will mind, because he," Puss reached for his sword, but remembered it was missing, "is me!"

"Oh, okay," Dog said.

"Normally I have a sword . . . it's like a whole thing, you know?" Puss said.

Then it dawned on Dog. "Pickles, *you're* Puss in Boots?"

"Not yet, but I will be," Puss said, determined to take upon—and earn—his mantle once more.

"I'll come with you!" Dog called, but Puss was already running into the woods.

"Sorry, perro! Puss in Boots walks alone!"

CHAPTER 7

Outside Jack Horner's pie factory, the Serpent Sisters Jo and Jan chatted with Jack's henchmen.

"Howdy, boys! We've got a special delivery for Mr. Jack Horner," Jo said.

Puss surveilled the area. He pulled himself up to the top of the wall to scout out Horner's headquarters. Although Puss had completed many missions before— perhaps far more dangerous ones—this was the first one without his extra lives to count on.

"Okay, just get in and out," Puss said, trying to give himself a pep talk. "Easy peasy."

"Lemon squeezy!" came a voice. Puss whipped around and saw Dog standing right next to him, a stick clenched in his mouth.

"*Ay*, Dios mio, what are you doing here?"

"I brought you a sword," Dog said.

Puss was ready to explode.

"That's not a sword; that's a stick," he said.

"It's a stick-sword!"

"Go home," Puss growled.

Puss turned his attention back to the factory. It was surrounded by massive, spiked gates and a team of rough-looking henchmen.

"My home is where my friends are," Dog said to Puss.

"Again, we are not friends," Puss reminded him.

Dog lifted his sweater up, revealing his belly. "Rub for luck?"

But Puss was only getting more annoyed. "I don't need luck for this," he said. "I am a highly skilled master cat thief. Watch."

Puss slid down into a small pie vent, but he accidentally got stuck halfway. As Puss shimmed himself into the vent, Dog slipped the stick in Puss's scabbard.

"You got this," Dog assured him.

Puss didn't reply. He shimmied his way down.

Inside the pie factory, a line of nervous bakers watched as a giant thumb came in and smashed into a pie, then lifted it up to teeth to taste.

Jack Horner was wearing an apron covered in strawberry jam. "I pronounce this batch . . . delicious," he said. "Ship 'em out."

When he was done taste-testing, the Serpent Sisters, came in with a box.

"Oh! The map to the wishing star. Now let's take this prize to the trophy room, hm?" Jack said.

"Well, I can tell you, this map wasn't easy to—"

Jack cut Jo off. "TAKE IT TO THE TROPHY ROOM!"

Moments later, Puss was still struggling in the vent. But he managed to slip out and land directly in the trophy room. He stepped away from the case only to be almost burned by a fire-breathing phoenix in its cage.

Jack entered the trophy room with the Serpent Sisters in tow. Puss watched as they looked around and gasped.

It surely was a sight to see—Jack's collection of magical objects filled tall shelves all around the room. Among the collection were more glass slippers, bottled fairies, a bunch of crystal balls, magical carpets, baby unicorn horns, the shrunken ship of the Lilliputians, and some sort of enchanted hammer. Little did Jack know, Puss was sneaking behind the objects, ready to make his move.

"These are all trinkets," Jack Horner explained. "They're *nothing* compared to the awesome power of the magic wishing star!"

The Serpent Sisters uncuffed themselves from the box and handed it to Jack. He set it on his desk and inserted a key in the lock, beaming greatly.

"You see, as a child I had very little magic in my life," Jack said. "I wasn't a little talking animal, I didn't have a fairy godmother, and I sure didn't live in no shoe. So much magic was in the world and none for me. But look at me now, the soon-to-be master of *all* magic!"

Like most evil villains are apt to do, Jack went down memory lane, recounting all of his childhood to the Serpent Sisters. He probably wouldn't have relived his childhood if he'd known Puss's plan. But alas! Jack had grown up as a baker's boy, but with all the magic in the world, he'd never feel powerless again.

From his perch above, Puss descended on the box. He opened it up and saw the folded map, glowing magnificently. "Easy peasy, lemon squeezy," Puss said to himself.

Puss was about to take it for himself when he realized something was clinging to the lid.

The something grabbed the map. Puss reeled it back.

"Puss?" the something said. And it wasn't just any something. He knew that voice. It was Kitty Softpaws, Puss's sometimes-partner whom he hadn't seen in *years*.

"This is my job," Puss said, yanking her sash and taking the map. The pair started arguing via whispers. Kitty pulled it back.

"No, this is *my* job. I'm double crossing the bears."

"No, *I'm* double-crossing the bears. They tried to hire me earlier today."

"Well, they tried to hire me two weeks ago. That makes you plan B." Then Kitty stared at Puss's scruffy beard.

"What's this? Are you a pirate now? It's like a possum crawled on your face and died. Of shame."

Puss shushed her. "Will you please mock me quietly," he whispered.

"I hate it. It's disgusting," said Kitty.

"Well, I love it. It's distinguished." Puss's pride already hurt—he really needed that map.

Just then, Puss heard something in the airducts above. It was Baby Bear falling through the ceiling, hitting a shelf on the way down and landing limp behind the desk.

Jack was now back to reality. "What the—?" he started to say.

But Baby Bear's rope and grappling hook followed, bonking him on the head. Goldilocks and the other bears stared through a hole in the ceiling.

"Great plan, Baby. Real cat-like," Goldilocks chided.

There was a brief moment where everyone—Jack, Kitty, Puss, Goldilocks, the Three Bears, and the Serpent Sisters—stopped to look at one another. Everyone knew each other by reputation, but not in the flesh. Having gotten paid, the Serpent Sisters fled the scene.

Goldilocks glanced at Puss in disbelief. "Puss in Boots?"

"Goldi. Bears," Puss acknowledged them.

"Hola, Jack," Kitty said casually.

Goldilocks turned to Kitty. "You said you were going on a spiritual retreat!" Then she looked back at Puss. "And YOU'RE supposed to be dead."

"Maybe he's a ghost," Baby Bear suggested.

"Now hand over that map," Goldilocks shot a threatening look at Jack.

"And throw in a dozen pies!" added Papa Bear. The bears were so excited about the pies—Mama wanted to make sure there were some savory options, and a bag to go, of course.

As the group fought over the map (and the pies), they heard a slow creak. One of Jack Horner's magical items—a ship—fell out of a bottle in the trophy room and the shelves started to collapse. All at once, each individual magical item and cabinet fell over, creating a smokescreen of pure chaos. Never one to miss an opportunity, Puss (with Kitty in tow) escaped on the magic carpet, out the back office, and onto the factory floor. He had the map!

"Hah!" Puss taunted Jack as they flew out.

"I hate talking fairy-tale animals," Jack Horner sighed.

Quickly, Jack met the pair on the factory floor with a crossbow loaded with a baby unicorn horn. The unicorn horn projectile hit the magic flying carpet and pinned it to a wall, knocking Puss and Kitty off and onto a conveyer belt, but Puss still had the map.

"Ha. The best thief has won," Puss said, taunting Kitty with the map.

"You're right. She did," Kitty said.

Puss then looked upon his adversary. Kitty had

managed to coax the map out of his grasp, and she was now running full speed ahead. Kitty easily jumped f rom baker to baker, pulling the hat over the eyes of one baker, then pulling and ripping off the mustache of another. She was an excellent fighter, and all her skills were on full display as Puss got his beard caught in the conveyer belt.

"Nice catching up with you, Puss! Gotta go," Kitty said as she flew out.

But the chase wasn't over yet. Still on the conveyer belt (and with no map, to boot), Goldilocks and the bears, still hot on the trail, descended upon him. Puss was terrified. With only one life left, if something happened to him on this mission, that was it.

Puss scrambled to find something to fight with and against the bears. Instinctively, he reached for his sword, but it wasn't there. It was just the stick that Dog had given him.

"Is that a stick? What are you going to do with a stick?" Baby Bear taunted him.

Puss threw it into his face.

"Ow!" Baby Bear yelped.

Then Puss caught it in midair and swatted Mama with it.

On the offense, Papa Bear launched Puss into the air, twirling him like a pinwheel. Then Puss slammed into Kitty, and both of them crashed through the window.

CHAPTER 8

Puss and Kitty landed in the bed of the luxurious carriage that transported the Serpent Sisters and the map, heaped with bags of gold. Dog popped up in the driver's seat.

"Hey, Puss, I found a sandwich in here! I think it's tuna fish—"

"Drive, perro!" Puss commanded. He knocked the sandwich out of Dog's paws.

Dog snapped the reigns, startling the horse into a full gallop. With Jack's henchmen on their tails, the carriage burst through a wall and into town, narrowly missing the arrows that Horner's guards aimed at them.

"Oh cool, another member of the team," Dog said, acknowledging Kitty.

"We are *not* a team!" both Puss and Kitty replied at the same time.

"Nice getaway driver," Kitty said to Puss. "Who is this guy?"

"I'm Puss's best friend," Dog replied for him.

"No, he isn't," said Puss.

"And his therapy dog!"

"Definitely not."

"Finally!" Kitty said. "You need therapy." (Therapy is a great tool for examining your thoughts and behavior— couldn't we all use some therapy?)

The carriage sped through a narrow street. Puss was now back to his original mission. "Give me the map. Trust me," he said.

"Trust you? Like I did in Santa Coloma?"

Puss couldn't believe Kitty would bring that up *here* of all places when it was anything but the time. (Not that he ever wanted to get into it with Kitty about Santa Coloma.) Thankfully, the task at hand quickly took their attention. The carriage tore through a marketplace, but the cats were too busy fighting over the map to notice what had transpired. Their cries of "mine!" turned into high-pitched yowls and hissing. And Horner's guards were gaining on them.

Puss looked at the bags of gold and got an idea. He kicked them from the back of the carriage, where they then broke open on the ground and spilled golden loot everywhere. A greedy crowd descended upon it, temporarily blocking the narrow bridge and stalling the rest of Jack Horner's henchmen.

"Good people! Accept these golden gifts from Puss in Boots," Puss called out. The crowd cheered for him; Puss, naturally, basked in the adoration.

But then Puss heard a familiar, eerie whistle break out from the crowd. As he turned, he froze in fear as he caught glimpse of the wolf standing among them.

"Speed up! Go, go, go!" Puss called to Dog.

The carriage raced off in the distance and Puss was happy to put as much distance between him and the wolf as possible.

Jack Horner was a man on a mission. With the map gone, he returned to his trophy room to gather everything he needed to reclaim it.

Into a magical, bottomless bag, he deposited Captain Hook's hook; a trident; a bandolier belt with poison apples; a crossbow with unicorn horns; a wizard's staff; jars of fairies and other creatures; a tiny, delicate potion bottle marked "Drink Me" and a cookie marked "Eat Me"; a sword in a stone; magic wands; jewelry; a crystal ball; and a whole shelf of other magical things.

Next, Jack Horner grabbed the fairy godmother's magic wand and slammed it into a pumpkin, transforming it into a heavily armored tank in which to ride.

Last, he outfitted himself with four hornless unicorns driving the tank, as well as thirteen rough henchmen, also known as "the Baker's Dozen." (A baker's dozen at a bakery means thirteen!)

Jack stared into one of his crystal balls, which showed him exactly where Puss and the map had gone.

Kitty, Puss, and Dog continued driving the carriage out of town. They broke the seal of the folded map and opened it with anticipation, but to Kitty's dismay, it was blank.

"Wait a minute, what is this? We've been ripped off! Where is the—?"

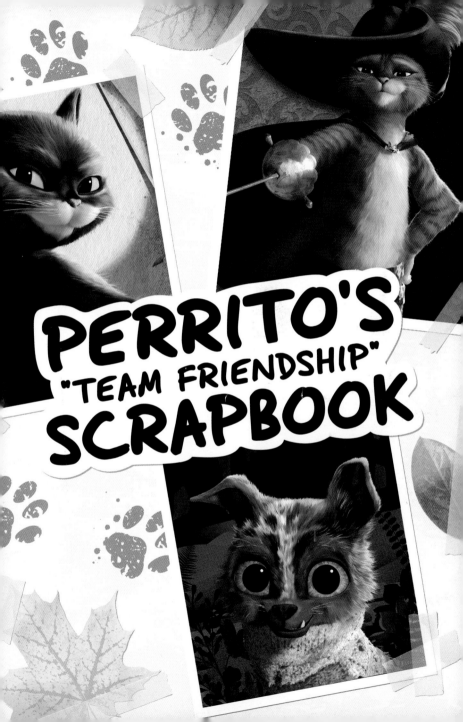

PERRITO'S
"TEAM FRIENDSHIP"
SCRAPBOOK

Hi there! I'm Dog. My friends call me Perrito. OK, maybe they wouldn't really call me their friend . . . not yet anyway! I'd like to make a "Team Friendship" scrapbook to document our time together. Did you know that when we're not ripping them up, dogs love scrapbooks? I mean, you get to put all your favorite things inside . . . pictures of your friends, artifacts from your travels . . . and in a moment of weakness you maybe even get to rip it up. (But try not to rip it up. Scrapbooks are FUN!)

By the way, if you haven't read our whole adventure, you might want to come back to my scrapbook at the end! I don't want to spoil anything for you.

I met Puss in Boots at Mama Luna's compound. Of course, at that time he was going by the name "Pickles" and I was, well, disguised as a cat! No one could tell I was a dog in my cat disguise, but Puss saw the real me. We became friends and I told him all about my dreams of becoming a therapy dog.

I knew that Pickles wasn't just another housecat. But I didn't know he was actually the legend, Puss in Boots! OK, he told me about the legend himself. And OK, I don't really care about the legend. But I care about Puss, and that's all that matters. And Puss was going on a mission to find a special map . . .

PICKLES

See this cool stick? I followed Puss on his journey to some pie factory—boy was he surprised to see me there! But as his friend, I couldn't let him go off on an adventure without a sword, could I? (He lost his before we met.) Okay, okay. The sword I gave him was actually this stick. But I still think it was helpful!

Inside the pie factory, Puss found Kitty Softpaws. They knew each other even longer than I knew Puss. She was there for the map, too! What are the odds? There was a bit of a kerfuffle inside the factory, but eventually Kitty and Puss appeared with their special map! Kitty was nice to me from the very start, and she's AMAZING at doing a cute-eye trick that can distract anyone . . .

Puss and Kitty fought about who got to hold the map, so I got to! I didn't care about the map. It didn't look particularly delicious to eat or fun to pee on, but I just wanted them to stop fighting.

But it turns out that the map led to the mysterious dark forest and it was actually wonderful. It wasn't dark at all! There were trees in all different colors, and magical stardust everywhere. Here's a posy from the field of flowers. It's dry now, but I'm going to keep it FOREVER!

On our journey through the forest, Puss and Kitty tried to teach me their cute-eyes trick. They are so adorable when they make those cute eyes! Then Puss asked Kitty to get rid of his beard—and, oh boy, he looked 10 years younger after that!

Also looking for the map were Goldilocks and the Three Bears. Goldilocks had a big stick-looking staff. Do you see it? I kind of wanted to chase it, but they also scared me, so I knew I couldn't. Just know that I wanted to. I REALLY wanted to chase that staff.

Later, I saw Puss run off into the forest with a scared look on his face. This was my moment to be a great friend and a great therapy dog. I ran after him, rested my head on his chest, and told him that it's okay to be scared. It was my first time being a true therapy dog, and I was so proud of myself! I even kept a little leaf from the forest floor where we were sitting, I never want to forget that moment.

Once Kitty found us, we knew we could find the wishing star by working together. This was when I first used the name "Team Friendship" to describe the three of us: me, Puss, and Kitty. Best friends! Although, the "Team Friendship" name wasn't Puss and Kitty's favorite at first.

Speaking of names, Kitty liked to call me "Perrito." I'd never had a name before, but it was starting to grow on me. Plus, I like that it kind of sounds like "purr," which Puss does when he's really focused on something!

Going through the mysterious dark forest was an amazing adventure, but even more amazing was getting to spend time with Puss and Kitty. I think they liked spending time together, too. They don't bristle so much at the name "Team Friendship" anymore! Speaking of names . . . since I liked it so much, Puss and Kitty gave me my very own name: Perrito!

Team Friendship forever!

Just then, words magically appeared.

"Oh yeah. I knew it was going to do that," Kitty said, trying to save herself.

Puss rolled his eyes at her and began to read. "The Dark Forest is deep and far. Within its bounds you'll find the star."

The words on the map changed, and Kitty read out loud: "A single wish burns true and bright. This map's the key, so hold on tight."

Realizing they were getting more information about the star, both Puss and Kitty attempted to take the map to get a closer look themselves. But it was no use: neither would let the other have it. Kitty drew her sword; Puss drew his stick.

"A stick? What happened to your sword?" Kitty asked.

Puss couldn't admit what had happened with the wolf, at least not to Kitty. "Got rid of it, you know. Made things too easy. I needed a challenge," Puss said.

"Yeah, you looked pretty challenged back there," Kitty said.

Since the cats were still fighting over who got to hold the map, Dog piped up. "I can hold it," he said.

"Yeah, right! What's your deal anyway? You run with the Chihuahuas?"

"I don't think so," Dog replied.

"I don't believe you," said Kitty. There was no way Puss would just let some random stray tag along, right?

"That's okay. As long as you believe in yourself."

Kitty looked confusedly at Puss, "is he deranged?"

Puss shrugged. "Clearly."

". . . What's your name?" Kitty asked.

"Oh, I've been called all kinds of things. Dog, Bad Dog, Stupid Dog, Hey You, You There, Get Out, Leave It, Drop it! Big Rat. Small Pig. Rat Face. Butt Nugget. You know. That sort of thing. But I've never had a name that really stuck, you know. And that belonged to me."

Kitty wasn't convinced. "Nice try. Classic con. No one's that nice. I don't trust you. But! I trust you more than I trust *him*," she said, directing her voice at Puss.

The trio continued their journey until they reached the edge of the Dark Forest. The horse that had carried them through stopped in front, neighed, and then ran away. Puss thought he was a coward.

At the edge of the Dark Forest was a solid, impenetrable wall of black, twisted oaks and coiled brambles studded with razor thorns. It wasn't exactly an inviting or friendly place to enter, but it had to be done.

Puss reached out with one paw to touch a tree. When he did, the whole area shimmered and vibrated, like a pond reflection rippled by a tossed stone.

"All together. We step through as one. Ready? One, two—after you," Puss said, kicking Dog into the magic mirage first.

"Wait, what?!" Dog called. He disappeared.

Puss waited a moment, and then asked, "Dog? Are you still alive?"

"Let's find out," Kitty said sarcastically as she jumped into the magic wall, yanking Puss in as well.

The trio fell into a rainbow-colored void, and they passed through the barrier of the Dark Forest. They screamed and locked hands as they traveled through the rainbow-colored void with hope that they'd make it to the other side in one piece.

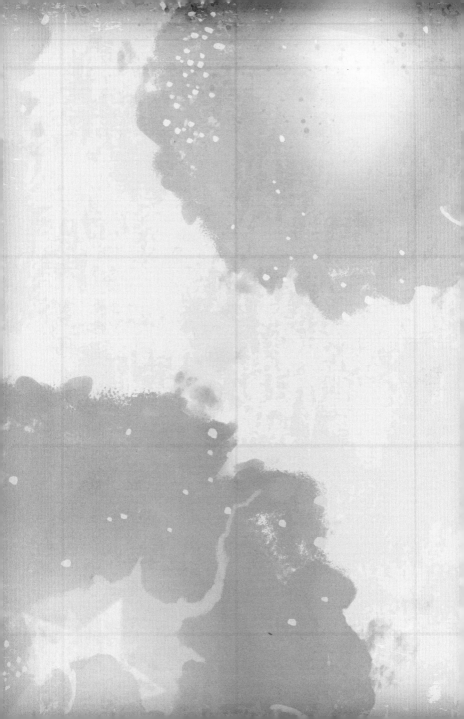

CHAPTER 9

Puss, Kitty, and Dog dropped out of the magic portal and out the other side. The trio officially made it into the Dark Forest, a place of enchantment born of the fallen star. It was magical and beautiful, full of technicolor trees and streams that sparkled with stardust—nothing like the name implied.

"Wow!" said dog in wonder.

"For a 'dark forest' this place is pretty colorful," Kitty added in awe.

"The wishing star is in here somewhere," said Puss determinedly. He turned to Kitty with a smile. "Kitty, may I please see the map?"

"No."

"Seriously? You won't even let me hold it for one minute?" said Puss.

"Not even for a second."

Puss lowered his head and took off his hat. "Come on, Kitty. You've got to *trust me*." Puss's eyes got huge with sudden cuteness, turning their adorable-yet-mighty power on Kitty.

"Wait, what's going on with his eyes?" Dog said. "Oh, they're getting bigger! Oh, Kitty you gotta trust him. Look at those eyes."

"You call that cute?" Kitty suddenly flashed her own cute-eyes at Puss; they were in a cute-eyes stand off!

Dog looked between them excitedly. "Oh! Look at her! Oh! Those eyes are even bigger than yours. Do whatever she wants, Puss."

The two continued to pull out their cutest faces and poses, charming Dog more than each other. "It's all. . . so. . .cute! Cuteness overload!" Dog exclaimed.

Suddenly, Dog fainted. Sprawled on the ground and groaning with exhaustion, Kitty and Puss finally relented, getting back to business.

"Can we look at the map now?" Puss said.

As they unrolled the map, magical stardust swirled over its surface, inscribing a rhyme in glittering script:

"*Follow this enchanted chart. It knows the path and knows your heart,*" Kitty read.

Two small avatars appeared on the map, clearly representing Puss, Kitty, and Dog at the edge of the forest. As Puss pointed at the avatars, the map suddenly adjusted into a customized path. And as they looked up, the forest around them adjusted, with rocks, trees, and topography creating a clear trail forward. *FWOOSH!* Flames suddenly ignited the borders of the trail.

The trio blinked, staring at the intimidating path.

"It says we must go through the Valley of Incineration, over Undertaker Ridge, through the Cave of Lost Souls. . . Really?" read Puss.

"Let me take a look," Kitty said as she pushed Puss out of the way. As she grabbed the map, enchanted dust rose from it and revealed a new path, once again customized to Kitty. Around them, the forest shifted again, this time into a bog of simmering acid.

"What?" Kitty said incredulously. "Swamp of Infinite Sorrows. Trust Falls, The Abyss of Eternal Loneliness? . . . There's something wrong with this map."

"I guess there's a different terrible path for everyone," Puss shrugged.

"It's almost like the forest doesn't want anyone to make a wish," said Kitty.

"I don't even have a wish, but can I try?" Dog asked. He stepped up to the map and stars filled his eyes. Then the map shimmered, and the forest switched once again, revealing a bright and new path.

"Ooh! Mine says we skip through the Pocket Full O'Posies," said Dog. "And then we drift down the Lazy River—that sounds fun!"

"No fair! Why does he get the good ones?" chirped Kitty with irritation.

"Wander the Field of Quick and Easy Solutions and arrive at the star. Oh wow! That sounds wonderful. Oh, but, no, no—this is your trip and I don't wanna impose."

Suddenly, avatars representing Goldi and the bears popped up on the edge of the map. Jack Horner's avatar popped up as well. Their enemies were gaining on them. The trio had to make a move *fast*.

"Uh, Pocket Full O'Posies sounds fun," said Puss. "Let's go!"

The Pocket Full O'Posies was exactly as described. Puss, Kitty, and Dog moved through a field of flowers.

"Birthday wish rules? What does that mean?" Dog asked curiously.

Puss and Kitty glanced at each other suspiciously, but Puss laughed it off.

"It means I'm not telling you my wish," he said.

"He doesn't want to tell us because it's something stupid. Like conditioner for that thing on his face," Kitty said.

"It's distinguished!" Puss replied indignantly.

"What about you, Kitty? What are you gonna wish for?" Dog asked eagerly.

Puss and Kitty shared another look. She wasn't going to tell, either.

"Can't tell you," she replied. "Birthday wish rules."

"Hah! I'll bet *your* wish is the stupid one—*OOF*!" A giant rose shot out of the ground, sending Kitty flying into the air, landing in full defense mode. Dog was oblivious and happily stopped to smell the giant flower.

"This must be 'Pocket Full O'Posies!'"

Puss leapt over Kitty, charging ahead as more flowers blocked his way.

"What? Whoa! Out of the way, demon flowers!" Puss cried in alarm.

Kitty pulled out her sword, determined to prune back the flowers. As she chopped one, two more instantly grew back in its place. As Puss and Kitty are knocked around by the giant roses, Dog keeps sniffing the flowers, which in turn nudge him along gently.

"I thought your path was supposed to be easy, Perro" Puss murmured.

"It is easy. I think all you have to do is stop and smell the roses," Dog said.

As the cats continued to struggle, Dog approached and took a big whiff of the bud that trapped Puss. It instantly lifted away.

"Don't rush through it. Take your time," Dog said, now freeing Kitty from her bouquet of flowers. "And really appreciate what's right in front of you."

"You're weird, Dog," Kitty said, although she was grateful to be free. "What exactly is your story?"

"My story? Oh! It's actually a very funny story. Back when I was a pup, me and my littermates lived with a family full of pranksters who liked to play hide-and-seek. And I was always 'it.' Pick on the little guy, am I right? But I'd always find them. They tried putting me in a packing crate, a dumpster . . . no matter how hard they tried, I'd ALWAYS find them. So, one day, they got creative, and they put me in a sock. With a rock in it! And then they threw me in a river! I gnawed a hole in the sock, and I swam to the surface. Never found them or my littermates, so I guess I'm still 'it'! Ha, ha, ha, ha." Dog continued to sniff the flowers.

"That is the saddest funny story I've ever heard. You of all people should have a wish," Kitty said.

"I already have a comfy sweater and two best friends. I've got everything I could wish for—*no magic required*."

Puss bristled at the word "friend," but it was showtime. Dog cleared the path, and it was time to keep moving.

While Puss, Kitty, and Dog made their way through Pocket Full O'Posies, Goldilocks and the three bears had also arrived. Goldilocks, gung ho on finding the wishing star, refused to tell her family what her wish would be.

"Will it make us big-time thieves?" asked Papa Bear

"Oh yeah, the biggest," Goldilocks replied.

"Will we get mad respect?" asked Baby Bear.

"Oh! The maddest!"

"That's my girl. Always looking out for the family," said Mama Bear, though she was starting to get suspicious as Goldilocks refused to reveal the exact nature of her wish.

"Oh! I can smell two cats and a dog. We're getting really close," said Baby Bear as they descended upon Pocket Full O'Posies.

"And I'm getting a whiff . . . of a pie?"

The bears look back to where a massive dust cloud has formed. With it was Jack Horner's tank and the Baker's Dozen. He wielded Excalibur, the sword still wedged in the stone.

"Well, if it isn't the folks who tried to steal from me," Jack sneered at Goldilocks and the bears. His tank pulled up alongside them and he swung Excalibur at Papa Bear. The stone crashed into Papa, sending Goldi flying as Papa collided with Mama and Baby.

"Blam! Haha!" Jack laughed maniacally at the sight of Goldilocks and the bears tumbling down the hill and out of sight. He turned to the Baker's Dozen, eager to revel in his success and show off Excalibur. "Yeah, I couldn't get this rock off it, but it's still pretty cool, right?"

CHAPTER 10

Jack's pumpkin tank charged ahead, aggressively mowing through flowers. He closed in on the Pocket Full O'Posies and did it fast. However, the giant roses that shot from the earth really put a *thorn* (see what we did there?) in his plans and blocked the way. The tank came to a violent stop.

Frustrated, Jack barked orders at his henchmen.

"Well? Start chopping!" Jack yelled.

The Baker's Dozen leapt to the forest floor and hacked away at the flowers. But suddenly, one tough baker's whole body got swallowed by a giant carnivorous daisy. Nothing but bones were left behind.

"Jerry! No!" called one of the other henchmen as Jerry's cleaver landed on the railing next to Jack.

Jack knew it was time to bring out the big guns. He buried his arm deep into the endless bag and pulled out the "Eat Me" cookie and "Drink Me" bottle.

"Ooh, magic snacks. Save those for later," Jack said, tossing them back in. He then pulled out a large spinning wheel and tossed it aside. Next, he pulled out a broom with little waving arms and tossed that aside, too.

"Guess I overpacked," Jack quipped. "Aha! Pay dirt!" From the inside of the bag, Jack produced a jar with a magical cricket inside.

"Defoliate! Fly and feast! Eat those flowers!" Jack called to the locust as its eerie glow bathed his face. But it wasn't a magic locust at all.

It was a cricket.

"What are you, then? Some sort of demon grasshopper? A deadly fairy? Put a spell on this forest, then."

"I don't cast spells!" said the bug.

"Well, what DO you do?"

"I—I judge you. I sit on your shoulder and judge your actions and the quality of your character. I'm like . . . an ethical bug!"

Jack grumbled.

"I really DID overpack," he said.

WHAM! A bearded baker slammed onto the tank next to Jack. The baker held on for dear life as a giant buttercup tried to pull him away.

"Aren't you gonna help him, Jack? You're losing a lot of men!" cried the bug.

Jack kept digging in the bag.

"I'm not really stressing about manpower, because in my bag are the mightiest fairy-tale weapons from my enchanted arsenal. These babies are gonna get me that magic wish even after the whole team is dead and gone." Jack admitted.

Bug winced. "Now, now, Jack, as your conscience, I think you should—"

Jack pulled out a beautiful red bird from his bag. It was a phoenix, a symbol of rebirth and the eternal circle of life. He clearly wasn't interested in having a conscience. Jack was all villain.

FWOOSH! Jack stretched the neck of the phoenix and aimed it like a flamethrower, igniting the forest. Some of his men screamed in agony as they were lit on fire, but Jack didn't care.

"Don't be near where I'm flame-throwing!" Jack called out. It wasn't his fault the Baker's Dozen weren't quick enough to get out of the way.

CHAPTER 11

Puss, Kitty, and Dog drifted down the Lazy River from Dog's map. True to the "lazy" name, they admired their adversaries' avatars on the enchanted map. Jack Horner's location was stuck in Pocket Full O'Posies.

"Do your job, demon flowers," Kitty said.

Meanwhile, Dog was practicing his cute-eyes trick. It wasn't going well.

"Okay, one more time. Like this," said Kitty as Dog watched her hypnotic cute-cat gaze intently. "Trust me," she continued, trying to lure him into the gaze.

"Aw. That's amazing. But of course, I trust you and Puss, even without the eyes," Dog said.

"Yeah? Big mistake," said Kitty.

"What do you mean? You're my friends."

"You know what trust gets you? A sock, a rock, and a swim in the river," Kitty replied.

"You have to trust *somebody*, right?" asked Dog.

Kitty shook her head. "Whenever I've let my guard down, I've been played, betrayed, and . . . declawed." Kitty looked down at her paw. "Never again. I'm a solo act. I keep my secrets, and I play my cards close. That's how you get a winning hand. Take it from me. Never trust *anybody*."

Kitty held up Dog's sweater vest. During her speech, she had expertly swiped it with her cat-thief skills, further demonstrating that he couldn't trust anybody. Dog, however, stared at her innocently, wagging his tail. He thought it was amazing. Kitty threw the sweater back at Dog with a grin.

While Kitty and Dog were contemplating the intricacies of the cute-eyes, Puss had a dilemma all on his own. It was the beard. He could pretend that he liked it all he wanted, but he didn't. So, maybe if he convinced Kitty to help him, he could spare his feelings and restore himself to his natural state all at once.

"Kitty, I've been thinking. My beautiful beard. It is very distinguished, yes, but it does deprive the world of a good look at . . . my face. So, if it will make you happy,

I could be convinced to—"

"I've gotten used to it," Kitty interjected.

"Wait, what?" This wasn't part of Puss's plan.

"The beard. Keep it."

"Well, you see . . . heh," Puss started to say, but he couldn't handle it anymore. "Kitty, PLEASE! Get this itchy thing off me!" He launched himself into another round of frenzied scratching.

"Hold on. Is the great Puss in Boots asking for *help*? Can't shave it yourself? Isn't your stick sharp enough?"

"Ha, ha! She's razzin' ya, Puss!" Dog called.

Kitty had her fun, but she wouldn't make Puss beg. She drew a small ankle knife from her boot and started shaving him aggressively. When she was done with her masterpiece, Puss had a long, swooping mustache that connected to very frizzy muttonchops.

Then she changed the style again and gave Puss a goatee with a mess of curls on his head.

Finally, Kitty decided to really finish up, trimming around Puss's throat.

"There's the handsome face I've been thinking about . . . punching," Kitty said.

"The face you haven't seen since . . . Santa Coloma," said Puss, realizing how long it had been since he'd felt like himself.

Puss put his cavalier hat back on, and Kitty noticed the scar above his brow. That was new. She handed him her ankle knife.

"Here. Consider this a souvenir," she said.

For Puss, it wasn't much of a knife, but it did beat a gnawed-up stick. Puss slipped the knife into his belt and chucked the stick away without a second thought.

But for dogs, a chucked stick is more than they could ever resist. Dog zeroed in on the flying stick. It was instinct. He had to have it. He bounded onto the shore, barking at the stick. Then he charged into a wall of foliage and disappeared.

Puss and Kitty, realizing the gravity of the situation, jumped off their boat and onto the shore, looking for him urgently. But before they had a chance to call Dog back, Jack Horner and his pumpkin tank plowed through the tree line, rolling up on Puss and Kitty. What's more, he had Dog in his grasp!

"Oh look, I found a little lost dog," Jack said. The Baker's Dozen (now down to about nine guys) burst from the forest, brandishing weapons and kitchenware. Kitty held up her own sword. Puss, on instinct, grabbed the map and clutched it tight.

"Let him go, Jack!" Kitty yelled.

"Oh, I don't know. I might keep him," said Jack. He reached into his endless bag and pulled out a crossbow loaded with a unicorn horn. Jack was angry that Puss and Kitty were trying so hard to get the wish. Jack aimed the unicorn horn in Dog's face. "Now, make with the map or we'll see what the unicorn horn really does."

"Why, you're not going to shoot a puppy are you, Jack?" Ethical Bug chimed in from Jack's shoulder.

"Yeah, in the face. Why?" Jack replied.

WHAM! Suddenly, one of the Baker's Dozen slammed into the side of Jack's tank, causing him to drop Dog. The attack came from none other than Goldilocks and the bears, all of them looking thrashed, trashed, and thoroughly angry.

"Give us the map, or the Baker man gets it!" Mama Bear called, threatening one of Jack's henchmen.

"I don't even have the map," Jack said. "Plus, I don't care about him. Just stop throwing my men at me!"

Taking advantage of the momentary pause, Dog made a break for it, leaping from the tank and scampering on the forest floor. He dodged through legs and avoided grasping hands as Jack's henchmen lunged for him.

Kitty turned to Puss, thrusting the map into his hands.

"First one to the dog gets the wish," she called out

playfully. Then she charged into the fray, sword in hand.

Meanwhile, Baby Bear and Papa Bear's attention diverted to Puss and the map. Papa Bear slammed a pillar of rocks at him, but Puss expertly dodged it, collapsing onto one of Jack's henchmen. From there, it was all eyes on Puss. He dodged a meat cleaver from one of Jack's men and diverted the unicorn horn into one of the Baker's Dozen, who instantly exploded into glitter.

After Puss dodged another of Jack's attacks, it hit one of the henchmen instead. The force of the glittery explosion flung Puss off, and the map flew out of his grasp. Just as Puss moved to retrieve it, he heard something.

A whistle.

Puss turned and saw the wolf standing on the river's far bank. Puss didn't have time to wonder how the wolf managed to track the group all the way there. The wolf's whistle pierced through any thought Puss had, reminding him of the fear that shook his core during their first meeting. The wolf reminded him of his mortality. How he wasn't indestructible. That the *true* death of the legendary Puss in Boots was imminent.

But Puss remained determined to stay alive, no matter the cost. So, as the wolf drew his scythes, Puss panicked and ran. Dog chased after him, too, but it was too late—Puss was gone.

Goldilocks nabbed the map and let out a loud bear roar. At last, she had the map! Her eyes glittered and the forest shifted yet again, this time from Dog's path to Goldilocks's.

As the dust cleared, Jack saw Goldilocks and the bears disappear into the distance with the map and his only chance to wish for enough magic to never feel powerless ever again.

CHAPTER 12

Puss ran as far and as quickly as he could from the shoreline. He wasn't exactly sure what running would accomplish. He just knew that he had to leave and escape the wolf no matter the cost. He took big, desperate gulps of air. He could feel his heart pump in his chest.

Puss's head swiveled around frantically, looking for the wolf in the trees. But in his nervous state, the wolf seemed to be *everywhere*. There was no escape from his fate. This was the end for Puss.

Panicking, Puss tripped over and landed on a branch in the dense and dead forest. He cowered back against the tree stump, panting hard and grabbing his chest as he realized the wolf hadn't actually followed. He was safe, for now, even though his body and mind thought he was still in some sort of danger.

In pursuit, Dog finally found Puss sprawled upon the forest floor, wild-eyed, breathing hard.

"Puss, what's wrong?" Dog asked. When Puss didn't reply, Dog instinctively rested his head on Puss's chest. Dog noticed that Puss continued to breathe rapidly.

Puss pet Dog until the moment of panic passed. Dog was really getting a hang of this therapy thing!

"Thank you, perrito," Puss said. On seeing Dog's confused and concerned expression, Puss knew it was time explain everything. "I am down to my last life. And I am afraid."

"It's okay to be afraid," said Dog.

"Not for Puss in Boots. I am supposed to be a fearless hero, a *legend*. But without lives to spare, I am nothing. I need that wish to get my lives back."

Dog thought about that for a second.

"You should talk to Kitty—"

"No, she cannot hear of this."

"Okay, but—"

"Kitty will never trust me again. Not after Santa Coloma. Santa Coloma wasn't a heist, perrito. It was a church. With a priest. And guests. And Kitty. And everything but me."

The event sunk in for dog. Puss and Kitty were supposed to be wed, but he had left her at the altar.

"It was wrong, I know. I am ashamed. I just wish I hadn't hurt her so badly," Puss said.

Little did Puss and Dog know, Kitty had arrived right when he started talking about Santa Coloma. She heard everything. And her heart sunk, too. Kitty had some confessions of her own.

Kitty entered the thick of things, and Puss admitted that he lost the map, but Kitty waved it off. She was very moved by what Puss had shared.

"We'll get the map back. We've been in worse pickles," she told him.

"Wait, who told you that name?" asked Puss.

"What name?"

"Oh, um. Nothing. Nevermind."

On the mountain trail, Goldilocks and the bears jogged toward the wishing star, their strides excited and upbeat.

"I can taste that wish now. Do you know what it tastes like?" Papa Bear asked.

"Pies?" guessed Baby Bear.

The bears broke out into a song over pies.

"Imagine us: a *big-time* crime syndicate," Papa Bear said gleefully.

"Not a big-time crime syndicate, love. A big-time crime *family*. Isn't that right, Goldi?" Mama Bear called out with glee. "Goldi?"

Goldilocks was distracted, but she looked up when Mama said her name. "Sure, sure, Mama. Everything will be just right."

The image on the map started to shift as the stardust churned and vibrated.

SHOOF! The stardust vacuumed into nothingness. The map was blank.

Baby Bear snatched it from Goldilocks, but she bit and battled him for it once more. "You're the smash, I'm the grab," Goldilocks reminded him. "I hold the map." As Goldilocks took it once more, ornate, cursive letters appeared around the map. Goldilocks read:

TO FIND YOUR WISH, ADJUST YOUR VIEW. WHAT YOU SEEK MAY BE RIGHT IN FRONT OF YOU.

Goldilocks and the bears looked up in front of a charming fairy-tale cottage. Smoke piped from the chimney.

"Look, look! Right in front of us," said Baby Bear, pointing to the cottage.

"It looks like our cabin back home! Could that be what we seek?" added Mama Bear.

But Goldilocks wasn't convinced. "You really think *our* cabin is in the middle of the Dark Forest?" she asked.

To find out for sure, Baby Bear gave it the old sniff test.

"Something's cooking," he announced.

"Well, we better investigate!" added Papa.

The inside of the cottage was rustic and super cozy, complete with overstuffed chairs, comfortable-looking beds, a fire in the hearth, and bowls of porridge left out to cool. Even the cupboard had jars full of honey.

Papa Bear sunk into his old armchair recliner. "Hello, my old friend. I have missed you so," he said to it, before promptly falling asleep.

Mama, meanwhile, found herself entranced by the porridge. "Look, Goldi! It's made just the way you like it."

"No matter how you make it, she doesn't like it," Baby Bear quipped.

Mama strolled around the cottage, reminiscing about things. But one of the team wasn't amused. Goldilocks.

"Stop it, all of you. Just stop! It's the forest playing tricks!" Goldilocks shrieked. "This isn't real. None of this is real."

However, before Goldilocks could say anymore, the fairy-tale book on the table, *Happily Ever After: Fairy-tale*

Stories, called her attention. She put her hand on it, in complete disbelief that it was real.

"Aw, that was your favorite book. You used to stare at it for hours," Mama Bear said.

Goldilocks opened the book to a page of a perfect fairy-tale family standing in front of a castle. There were two human parents and a little girl in the middle. As she looked at the book, the magic of the forest played out a little scene. Stardust Goldilocks jumping on the bed. Stardust Baby Bear looking annoyed.

Goldilocks was confused why the forest would show her this, but for Mama Bear, the significance was clear.

"This was it," Mama Bear said suddenly, glancing around the cottage. "The day you found us. This was the day when *our* world became *just right*."

CHAPTER 13

Dog glared up into the trees. Puss and Kitty had climbed up into the forest canopy, using the branches like the rungs of a ladder, and left him behind on the forest floor. (Okay, sure! Dog couldn't exactly climb trees, but RUDE!)

As Puss tried to look through the canopy, the branch he was latched onto broke. Puss swung into a plunging drop, but in a lightning-fast move, Kitty grabbed on and made sure he was okay.

"If you wanted to hold my hand, all you had to do is ask," Kitty quipped.

"Um. Just. Feel free to pull me up whenever you get the chance."

"Oh, I was just remembering the last time I offered you my hand. Only, *that* time I believe you had cold feet."

Puss smiled weakly as Kitty finally pulled him back up. Now they were both on the same side of the tree, standing whisker-to-whisker.

"Well, since we're on the topic . . . Kitty, um. I am sorry about Santa Coloma. It was wrong, it was cowardly, and I should have apologized for it long ago," Puss said.

"Don't eat yourself up too much," Kitty said. "I didn't show up either."

Puss blinked, taking this in. Kitty climbed higher, leaving him behind.

"Wait, *what*?" Puss asked. He scrambled up the tree after her, but she popped up on random branches, as if taunting him.

"I know I could never compete with your one true love," Kitty admitted. "'The legend.'" Kitty pulled the brim of Puss's hat down on his face before pulling it off him entirely. "I wasn't going to show up for that guy. But you don't seem like the same guy anymore." She put his hat on her head. Then she smirked and climbed off.

Puss pondered for a moment what that all that meant, before turning back to the task at hand. After a bit more climbing, Kitty and Puss came across a vast horizon of magical snow flurries and chimney smoke rising from the tree line. They traveled back down to the forest floor and told Dog their heading.

Kitty, Puss, and Dog approached the cottage warily, like commandos on a mission behind enemy lines (which, to be clear, wasn't *unlike* what they were doing). Puss would take the window; Kitty, the chimney; Dog, stay and watch guard.

Dog stuck out his paw. "Hands in, crew," he said, ready for a team handshake. "Ready, set, go, TEAM FRIENDSHIP!"

Puss and Kitty liked Dog a lot more than they did back in the carriage, but the name was a bit much.

"Team Friendship? I did not agree to this," Puss said.

"Just a placeholder name, you know. I'll workshop it. I'll bring back some other ideas," Dog replied. "Now. Go get 'em, tiger."

Dog gave Puss a slap on the rear, like a motivating team coach. (Though, Dog really should have asked for permission. Ground rules, folks.) "You can DO this."

Puss repeated that to himself as entered the cottage. He *could* do this. After all, he was the legendary Puss in Boots! He inched open the window of the cottage and took stock.

Baby had dozed off, his head resting on the table beside an empty jar of honey. Puss slipped inside just as Kitty made an acrobatic entrance through the chimney.

Puss held onto a hanging lamp. Beneath him was the table, Baby Bear, and, most importantly, the map. With quite a bit of gusto, Puss dropped to the table, crawled through the sticky honey mess, and snatched the map, leaving yellow pawprints all over the table.

Meanwhile, Mama and Goldilocks chatted in another room of the cabin.

"Goldi, I don't know what your 'just right' world means, I just hope we—" Mama started to say. Upon hearing their voices, Puss darted under the chair.

"Mama, it's, it's—"

Goldilocks was about to explain, but she glanced at the table and noticed the map was gone! She slammed her staff into the puddle of honey and sweat on the table. "Someone's nicked the map! Somebody took it!"

Goldilocks suddenly kicked over the chair that Puss was hiding under.

"Heh. Hola . . ." Puss started to say.

"Oi! You criming us? When we just crimed *you*? No crime backs!" Baby Bear shouted.

Goldilocks's rage exploded—how dare Puss jeopardize her wish?! She swatted at the map with her staff. It wafted through the air and landed on the honey-covered table.

Like lightning, Puss went to retrieve it, but Kitty dove onto the table from her perch. The pair tried to grab the map but accidentally grabbed one another's hands. Since Puss's paws were sticky with honey, their hands became stuck together.

Sealed paw-to-paw, Puss and Kitty stood over the map as the bears surged toward them. Kitty pulled Puss closer as the bears closed in. She had one move left, and she was ready!

"Let's dance," Kitty told Puss. Kitty twirled Puss around like a ballroom dancer. She dipped him, and Puss used that move to kick the hot porridge into Mama Bear's face.

YOW!

"Ahh! Too hot!" called Mama Bear.

Next, Kitty kicked a bowl of nearly frozen cold porridge in Baby's open mouth. It smacked him with a *CLUNK!*, taking him out, too.

"Ah! It's too cold! Brain freeze!" yelled Baby.

Puss stomped on one of the planks on the table, sending one last bowl of porridge wheeling through the air. Papa caught it and gulped it down. He softened.

"Ah," said Papa Bear blissfully. "This is just right."

With the bears temporarily out of the picture, Puss and Kitty looked into each other's eyes, continuing to spin.

Goldi, however, had other plans. Using her staff, she separated the cats. Though she successfully hooked the map, Kitty clung to it. As Puss flew in to attack Goldi, Kitty grabbed the map, unraveling it. Her eyes turned to stars. She'd activated *her* map!

Since Kitty had possession of the map, the cottage itself quickly splintered apart, opening a path down the center of the cottage. As Goldilocks realized she'd lost control, she reached out and grabbed the map, too.

The cabin responded in flux. The objects inside were suspended and floating, as if the new path idled between the two map-bearers.

At last, Dog darted in to help Puss and Kitty. Abruptly, Goldi grabbed a burning beam to throw at Kitty, but she dodged it. Like navigating a zero-gravity asteroid belt, Puss bounced along floating furniture and debris toward Kitty and Goldi. Papa Bear followed until his armchair flew through and dragged him in the other direction. With the others indisposed, only Goldi and Kitty remained fighting for the map.

"Team Friendship!" Dog hollered as he landed on Goldi's face, causing her to let go of the map, once and for all.

Kitty used the distraction to grab it and save Puss. She

even landed safely on the mantle. (After all, cats always land on their feet!)

The cabin started to come apart again and opened Kitty's path to Trust Falls. Mountains spiked through the earth and created a canyon. As the pieces of the cottage fell toward the ground, the spikes of earth grew into a mountaintop to meet them. Puss and Kitty clasped paws— was this the end?

Finally, the scene calmed down, and the team landed.

"We did it!" Kitty yelped.

"We have the map!" added Puss.

The mountaintop split and divided the cats and the bears. They ended up on two separate prongs of land, rapidly moving apart.

But one thing was missing . . .

"Oi!" Goldilocks called into the distance. "Forgot something?" She held up Dog, who was getting petted.

"Team. Avenge me!" Dog called out. He didn't want to be found. Not until they were victorious, anyway.

CHAPTER 14

Kitty and Puss pulled up the map to see where Dog's—and the others'—avatars were.

"Okay, they're at Trust Falls," Puss said, holding it up.

But only then did he realize. He was the one holding the map! It warped and suddenly their surroundings changed again. The Cave of Reflection appeared next to Puss and Kitty, right from Puss's path to the wishing star. *SHHHHK!* The ground shook as huge spears of crystal shot up from the crust of the earth.

Before Puss could react, Kitty fell to the ground as boulders stacked up magically, forming a canopy of stone. Meanwhile, a crystal cave formed around him, cutting him off from Kitty.

Divided by the wall of translucent, unbreakable crystal, there wasn't much else to do. Puss and Kitty locked eyes through the barrier, their hands pressed against it.

"You go find perrito. I'll find a way out of here," Puss told Kitty. They locked each other's gaze from between the crystal barrier—the last time they parted ways, things didn't end well. Would this time be different?

Kitty nodded before running off into the forest.

But little did Puss or Kitty know, Jack Horner had been watching them the whole time . . . with his crystal ball!

The journey through the Dark Forest had clearly taken a toll on Jack. He was sweaty and frazzled. He lashed his unicorns—and occasionally his men—with a horsewhip. In fact, he was down to the last two members of the Baker's Dozen and Ethical Bug on his shoulder.

"C'mon, hurry up! I'm not paying you to stroll."

"Listen, Jack," Bug started. "You're not growing as a *person*. It's like—like you've got a hole in your heart that nothing can ever fill."

"Nothing? I beg to differ, Ethical Bug." Sighing, Jack continued. "Do you know why Little Jack Horner sat in a corner?"

"Uh. . . because it rhymes?"

"Yeah, because it rhymes. That's true. But also: I sat in that corner because I was staring at the door. Waiting for happiness to walk through. It never did." Jack continued, "But then I realized: there is one thing that could make me truly happy."

"What's that?" asked Bug.

"Everything. All of the magic. Is that so much?"

That's your wish? What's that mean for everyone else?"

Jack smiled maniacally. "Take a look," he said. He held up a crystal ball, which showed a castle engulfed in flames, creatures all around running away in panic. The scene shifted to Puss and Kitty, turning back into regular feral alley cats, the magic being drawn out of them.

"When I get my wish, the whole world will be under my thumb," said Jack. "There will be no magic for anyone. Except me."

"Sweet Mother of Goose, Jack, your wish is horrible. Well, that means no more dreams come true," Bug replied, his voice shaking.

However, as Jack's unicorns trudged through the swamp, flowers on lily pads sprayed magical dust onto them. The unicorns sparkled with enchantment and sprouted new horns and giant wings. They then flapped up into the air and flew away.

"Stop them! Grab a hoof. Grab a fetlock. Grab onto SOMETHING, you dummy!" Jack yelled to his penultimate baker.

The baker reached into the air and seized one of the unicorn's legs. It was no use—he was taken skyward with the unicorn. *PLOP!* He fell to his death.

"You know Jack, perhaps this is the universe's way of telling you to—"

Jack impatiently reached up to his shoulder and flicked Ethical Bug away.

Jack turned to his last remaining baker and motioned toward the pumpkin tank. "You can pull this thing, right?" he said. "You're a survivor."

Back in the Cave of Reflection, Puss found himself surrounded by the cave's facets. Each one of them showed his reflection. Puss saw multiple images of himself, vanishing into infinity. And he could hear whispers . . . whispers calling his name!

Puss entered a vast stone chamber and gazed upon his reflection in a crystal pillar. This reflection was HUGE, certainly larger than life. As Puss looked at it, the reflection winked at him and tipped his hat!

Puss yelped out of fright and backpedaled right into another column. Just like that, a second larger-than-life Puss stared down at him.

"Why so jumpy, amigo?" this reflection asked.

Puss scrambled farther into the chamber, where he was met not by one or two Puss reflections, but *eight*. They were giant, boisterous, and they laughed, played music, and danced, just like the real Puss would. They each had eight distinct personalities and appearances: Gambler Puss, Guitarist Puss, Vanity Puss, Dancing Puss, Burly Puss, Swordsman Puss, Gold-Tossing Puss, and Tipsy Puss.

"Hello, Puss! Long time no see," called the swordsman.

"Always a pleasure to see me!" chimed Gambler.

"Hola, Number Nine!" sung the guitarist.

Now Puss understood. These columns weren't just random. They were his former *lives*! And then there he was, on his sole, last one.

"So, you're my former lives?" Puss asked, incredulous.

"Reflections of the good ole days," replied Vanity Puss.

"Back when we were larger than life," added Puss the swordsman.

Then the guitarist started to sing. "Who is your favorite fearless hero? Who is brave and ready for trouble?"

"We are! We are," cried all the versions of Puss.

Kitty was having a strange time as well. She snuck over to a ridge in this new map, where she caught wind of Goldilocks and the three bears. They were crossing over a fallen log in the Dark Forest, trying to forge a new path. Kitty could also see Goldilocks petting Dog. It seemed like the pets were quite aggressive. Kitty never pegged Goldilocks for a dog lover, so this was quite strange indeed.

"Well, that's it. Game over, innit? Them cats stole the stolen map we stole, and we ended up with diddly squat," Papa Bear said glumly.

Mama Bear wasn't as distraught. "Well, maybe we could be happy without a wish."

"No," Goldilocks interrupted her. "They'll come back for him." She held Dog up like he was a prized possession.

"You're darn tootin'. Puss and Kitty always rescue me when I'm kidnapped—which happens a lot—because we're a TEAM," said Dog. "Team Friendship. Well, we're still workshopping the name."

As the bears chattered and poked fun at each other, Kitty grabbed a massive pinecone and assessed its weight in her paws. Then she broke off a nearby branch, leaving her with a jagged spike. She jammed it into the pinecone. Her plan was ready!

"Speaking from one orphan to another, Goldi . . . you hit the jackpot. I wish I had a family like this. I mean, what else do you need in life?" Dog asked.

Goldilocks took a moment to think about this.

Mama, overwhelmed by how sweet Dog was to them, took Dog in her hands, cradling him. But when she looked back down at him, he had been replaced by Kitty's pinecone. There was even a note that read:

YOU'VE BEEN CRIMED! —KITTY

Kitty had secretly stolen Dog back, right out from under their noses!

CHAPTER 15

"**O**ne more number!" Guitarist Puss laughed to his other lives. But Puss couldn't.

"This has been fun, but can you tell me how to get out of here? I've got to get back to Dog and Kitty."

The music stopped. All the other lives blinked at Puss.

"Whoa. I thought you were going to get the wish. You got the map. You don't need them," said the swordsman.

"Kitty? I thought that was over?" Burly said.

"Yeah, we ended that at Santa Coloma."

"Ha, ha, ha! Santa Coloma." All of Puss's lives laughed. All of them, of course, except for one.

"Santa Coloma wasn't exactly our finest moment," Puss said sheepishly.

"What are you talking about? Puss in Boots walks alone!" chimed Tipsy.

"Town to town. No one could catch us, tie us up, or pin us down."

"Not even Kitty Softpaws. Right, amigos?"

The former lives reached in for a group high five. But Puss still wasn't feeling it. After all, he felt terrible for what he did to Kitty and wondered about the future they could have had.

"Come on. Was the legend so big that there was no room for anyone else? Not even Kitty?" he asked.

"The legend is STILL big, gato. It's YOU that got small," chirped Gambler.

"You changed, man," said Vanity.

"I hear he's best friends with a *dog* now. A dog he couldn't even protect from a couple of bears!"

"Pfft. Some hero. You have become a scaredy cat!"

The eight lives continued chiding and chastising Puss, but he'd no longer have it. For so long, he let the legend of Puss in Boots dictate what he did. Now that he was paw-to-paw with each one of them, the legend didn't feel so great.

"You know what? You guys are jerks, which is very conflicting for me. I'll find my own way out," Puss sneered as he turned away.

"Get out of here, Wuss in Boots," said the guitarist.

"Yeah, you smell like flop sweat and cheap cologne!"

"That's not cologne," Vanity said, sniffing the air. "That's the smell of—"

"Fear," said another, more menacing voice.

Out from the shadowy darkness, the wolf crept forward. Puss gasped in disbelief.

"I do love the smell of fear," the wolf sniffed. "It's IN-TOXICATING."

SMASH! In a flash, the wolf drew his sickles and shattered Tipsy's column with a single blow.

"Sorry to crash the party with your past lives—or your past *deaths*, as I like to call them," the wolf said. Then he shattered two more. "I was there to witness all of them. Each frivolous, untimely end."

The wolf receded into the darkness, leaving Puss trembling. He reappeared next to the remaining Puss lives.

"But you didn't even notice me. Because Puss in Boots laughs in the face of death. Right?" He shattered the column of Guitarist Puss. "But you're not laughing now." *SMASH!* There went Dancing Puss.

Now things started to click for Puss. The wolf wasn't just a wolf. And the wolf wasn't just a bounty hunter.

The wolf was . . . *SMASH! Death.*

The sad reality of the situation sunk in. Puss was not immortal. Not even a little bit.

"And I don't mean it metaphorically or rhetorically. Or poetically or theoretically or in any other fancy way," the wolf said, looming over Puss. "I'm Death, straight-up. And I've come for you, Puss in Boots."

The wolf continued his monologue.

"You know, I'm not a cat person. I find this very idea of nine lives . . . absurd," the wolf continued. "And you didn't value any of them. So why don't I do us both a favor and take this last one now?"

"That's cheating!" called the swordsman.

SMASH! The wolf took out Swordsman Puss, too.

The last Puss life, Vanity, desperately yelled, "Run, Puss in Boots! Get the wish!" *SMASH!* The wolf took him out too.

"Go ahead. Run for it. Makes it more fun for me," said the wolf.

Puss didn't know what else to do. So he followed Vanity's plea. Puss ran. He raced through the cave, desperately looking for a way out. As he frantically searched, the wolf's inescapable shadow loomed behind him.

The wolf's reflections surrounded Puss until finally he saw the light at the end of the crystal tunnel. He leapt toward the exit, but the wolf grabbed the edge of his cape, pulling him back. Puss desperately tried to keep moving forward as the wolf pulled and pulled and pulled until—

ZIP! The cape ripped, allowing Puss to make it through the exit and back out into the Dark Forest.

On the other side, Puss emerged in a sprint. He could barely think—he just had to run!

"Hey, Puss!" called Dog, who was also looking for Puss at the mountaintop. "Puss! Puss, we're here!"

Consumed with fear, Puss kept running. Kitty slowed to a halt at the start of the ridge. Her smile faded as Puss left them behind. She could tell that something was not right. What had happened to Puss?

Through the Dark Forest, Puss continued to run, looking back desperately to make sure the wolf was not following. He wouldn't squander this life—he wouldn't squander ANY more lives—he just had to outrun the inevitable, if the wolf was inevitable!

Puss ran so fast that he reached the edge of the forest in no time. This made him pause, as what lay before him was awesome. It was a giant crater with the wishing star at its center.

In his fear, Puss had done it. He had finally reached the wishing star!

The star was massive. It shimmered with magical power. Its surface was pure silver. As Puss neared it, he kicked up stardust.

Puss wasn't sure what to do. But it seemed the wolf

hadn't pursued him further. Uncertainly, he opened the enchanted map, and a sparkling incantation appeared, drawn in glittering cursive script. The star itself began to respond to the map, its points carving through the crater around it as it continued to rise.

Behold, Puss thought to himself. *The wishing star*.

And it was all his.

CHAPTER 16

Goldilocks and the bears traipsed through the forest, exhausted and worn.

"That's the third time we've passed the same rock, Baby," Goldilocks said.

"What do you want me to do? I've lost the scent," Baby complained with a cry.

"You only have one job; the one thing that makes you mildly useful is your nose, and apparently you can't even use that!" Goldilocks cried.

"I'm starting to think your 'just right' isn't what you promised us. So, what is it, Goldi? What's the wish?" Baby asked. "What's so blasted important that you've got us stranded in this haunted forest?"

The siblings were at each other's throats. Goldilocks couldn't take it anymore. She snapped.

"I'm getting a family, that's what! A *proper* family. Then everything will be just right!"

Goldilocks's words hung in the air. They stung. Baby, who argued with his sister frequently, felt shocked and hurt. Papa was flabbergasted. But Mama seemed to almost suspect it. Her face was unwavering.

"Just right is . . . getting rid of us?" Baby asked. He knew the answer, but he needed it confirmed.

"I'm not a bear," Goldilocks reminded them.

As the family processed the gravity of Goldi's statement, a rumble crashed in the distance, followed by a bright light skyrocketing way above the tree line. The family looked in its direction, in awe of what must be the wishing star.

"I was always afraid it was too good to last," Mama Bear said sadly. "And whether you think we're your family or not, if this is something that will make you happy . . . we'll get you that wish." She motioned solemnly to Papa and Baby. "Come on, boys."

With the star fully illuminated, and the motivation of the wolf beside him, Puss began to read the incantation.

"Star light, star bright, first star I see tonight . . ."

But Puss didn't finish the incantation. He heard a voice—Kitty's voice.

"I can't believe I fell for it again," she said, less conversationally and more to herself. She was at the edge of the star, standing with Dog.

This was it. Puss felt terrible. "Kitty! You don't understand." *She couldn't.*

"Don't understand what? That you've been playing me this whole time?" Kitty asked. "You want to know what MY wish was? One person, just one person, I could trust. In my whole life, I've never had anyone. Finally, here, I thought I found that person. Without a wish. I thought it was YOU."

Puss listened to Kitty's confession, feeling quite shocked to hear how she felt.

"Pretty stupid, huh? Same old Puss in Boots," she said.

These words stung. This Puss wasn't anything like the other eight lives he'd lived—the ones that laughed about Santa Coloma. No, he cared about Kitty. And a part of him cared about Dog. But she didn't understand. He had to make her.

"But I'm not! I'm not Puss in Boots! I'm . . . I'm on my last life! I need to get my lives back. Without them I'm . . . I'm not—" Puss could barely squeak the words out. They felt like a betrayal to his very core.

"What? The *legend*?" Kitty asked, mocking him. She shook her head, disappointed. "Huh. I still can't compete with your one true love." At least for Kitty, this was confirmation that she'd gone down the right path—until now, anyway. "Go on. Get your lives back, Puss in Boots. Just keep them out of mine."

And with that, Kitty Softpaws turned on her heel and stormed off.

Dog, too, looked at Puss. The disappointment was evident on his face. Then he followed Kitty.

"Kitty, I'm sorry. Death is after me!" Puss tried to reason. His explanation was enough to make Kitty stop in bewilderment, but that was short-lived.

Jack Horner had burst onto the scene!

"I've been called a lot of things!" Jack yelled. He had with him his magical bottomless bag, the last man of his Baker's Dozen, and a rolling pin with nails on it. His eyes furrowed and focused on the wishing star. "But never 'death.' I like it. That's MY wish."

Meanwhile, the bears also arrived. "That's *Goldi's* wish!" Mama Bear said.

Everyone had arrived, this time for a final standoff, all for the wishing star. There they were, the world's greatest thieves—Kitty, Puss, Goldilocks, the three bears, and Jack (plus the member of the Baker's Dozen and Dog, although they could hardly be considered thieves). At long last, they'd converged on the ultimate enchanted prize: the one, the only, legendary wishing star!

CHAPTER 17

*C*harge! Everyone made a beeline toward the center of the star . . . and right at Puss. He watched helplessly, sweating, as Kitty blocked Goldilocks in the nick of time to parry blows and blunt attacks, saving Puss. Kitty may have been angry at Puss, but she certainly didn't want him dead.

Almost overpowered by the brute force, Puss dropped the map. It blew across the surface of the star and near Baby Bear's paws.

But Dog swept in and tripped Baby before he could grab the map.

The melee ramped up into a torrent of action. Kitty and Goldilocks dueled once more; meanwhile, Puss had to fight and dodge the bears. Jack aimed his staff at Kitty and used its blaster power, which shot bolts of rapid-fire magic at her. *Bang! Bang! Bang!*

Kitty expertly dodged the attack, both jumping and ducking out of the way. As the calamity ensued, the wishing star continued to ascend. The magic got stronger as waves of cosmic power broke over the star's surface and swirled at its edges, drawing objects in its wake toward it. One of those things happened to be Jack's last baker henchman, who was pulled through the air and toward the wall of magic.

"Mister Horner! I need help," the final baker called out.

"Duly noted, but a little busy at the moment," replied Jack Horner, who aimed his staff at the others moving closer to the wishing star.

The baker's body started distorting and elongating, being pulled closer into the star magic.

BZZRT! The wall of magic pulled the last henchman into itself, and whatever-his-name-was dissolved into magical dust.

Puss dodged an attack from Papa Bear's claw and leapt to attack. But Papa Bear expected this and punched Puss in the air. Puss rocketed toward edge of the star, and he thankfully grasped the edge and saved his cavalier hat from flying away (that could have been bad)! Meanwhile,

Jack Horner saw the map and leapt for it . . . but Dog quickly rushed in and grabbed it with his mouth. Dog then ran with the fastest speed he could muster.

Still, it wasn't fast enough. Jack took this opportunity to grab Dog, steal the map, and fling Dog aside. Kitty caught him by the sweater.

The map changed hands (er, paws?) once more—this time, Mama Bear grabbed it. Jack turned up the strength of his magic staff and zapped Baby Bear off his feet and into the air. Baby tumbled through the air, drawn by some invisible force into the unbound magic at the edges of the star.

"Baby!" Mama Bear cried out. Seeing her baby about to be pulled into the wall of magic, Mama Bear grabbed onto his foot. But then she, too, started getting pulled in.

Papa noticed this and joined them, grabbing Mama Bear's foot. This was still no good, though—the entire bear family was being drawn in together, linked like a daisy chain on a string. They were doomed!

After a few more swipes from Kitty, the map found itself directly in Goldilock's range. This was her opportunity, her moment, what Goldilocks had been waiting a lifetime for. But just as she was about the grab the map, she saw Baby being stretched like taffy at the star's edge. Then she saw Mama Bear, then Papa Bear . . .

Goldilocks knew what she had to do. She let the map waft away as she ran toward the bears. She grabbed onto Papa's foot with all her might just as he started to levitate into the magic.

"Like I told you, Baby. You're the smash. I'm the grab," Goldilocks said, smiling. She wasn't going to let her family slip away—not without a fight!

With a supernatural strength, Goldilocks pulled the bears to safety. They tumbled onto the star's surface and fell into a big, furry pile—Goldilocks included.

Meanwhile, Jack picked up the map. Kitty leapt forward and kicked him in the face, which forced him to drop it once again. The two sparred, clashing with quick and mighty blows: Kitty's deadly blades crossing against Jack's magic staff.

Of course, while this duel took place, the map floated away. Dog chased it down, sliding to a stop in front of Puss, who was beside himself.

Dog slid the map over to Puss.

"Yeah. I don't know what to do with this. But if you think you need it—"

"Thank you, perrito," Puss said.

But Dog wasn't done. He surveyed the chaos around them and knew he had to say something.

"You know, I don't understand the whole nine lives thing. I've only ever had one life. But sharing it with you and Kitty has made it pretty special. Maybe one life is enough." Dog looked at Puss pleadingly.

Puss thought about that for a moment. He saw Goldilocks piled together with the bears, embracing one another in relief over what they could have lost. He saw Kitty furiously fighting Jack . . . maybe to protect Dog, maybe to even protect *him*, despite how they left things. And that led Puss to one conclusion.

Maybe Dog was right. Maybe there was a Puss with just one life left to live, greater than any legend that had come before.

CHAPTER 18

Weeeee-oooo.

A haunting whistle pierced through the scene, seemingly from nowhere.

The whistle was so harsh that even Kitty and Jack, who were fighting in a chokehold, looked up briefly upon hearing it.

But Puss saw him first. The wolf. *Death*. The wolf stepped through the curtain of magic at the star's edge, seeming bigger and stronger than ever, with his deadly sickles at his side—and Puss knew exactly what it meant.

"He's here for me," Puss said.

The wolf dragged his sickles across the surface of the

star, which prompted screens of light to rise from the star's surface that separated Puss from the others. It was Puss versus Death, how it was always meant to be. Although Puss was the one holding the map, he knew that he was trapped by the wolf.

Kitty's eyes widened. Hearing Puss's fear was one thing, but seeing the wolf stalk toward Puss like a predator was something else entirely. She finally understood the danger that Puss was in.

"I've enjoyed the chase, gato. But I think we've reached the end now, you and I," the wolf said, teeth bared.

Puss tried to continue the wishing star incantation, but the wolf sneered at him.

"Are you going to take the coward's way out? Or are you going to fight?"

CLANK! The wolf tossed something heavy and shiny to Puss. It was Puss's sword!

Puss's breath hitched as he struggled to continue the incantation, but, in this pivotal moment, he couldn't help but think about his past. His memories rushed forward, overriding any fear he felt, and he saw himself as he truly was . . . Puss as a kitten. Puss getting his boots. Meeting Dog. Reuniting with Kitty. Escaping with Dog. Showing Dog the super-cute eyes. Dancing with Kitty. Smelling roses with Dog . . .

"What's the matter, Puss? Lives flashing before your eyes?" the wolf sneered.

For once, Puss had an answer. He looked up at the wolf and smiled.

"No," Puss admitted. "Just one."

This was it! This was Puss's moment. He dropped the map, kicked up his sword, and fully accepted the wolf's challenge. He was ready to face Death. Not with no lives to spare, but with the only life that mattered.

"Fear me. If you dare," Puss declared with more energy and life than ever before as starlight swirled around them.

"This is going to be fun," the wolf replied.

The wolf charged as Puss sprang into the air. Steel met steel as they blocked each other's blows in an even match. Puss cartwheeled over the wolf's head, landing on the star's surface. Then he rushed at the wolf again.

Clash after clash, Puss finally managed to knock the wolf back. But it was hardly a winning blow—the wolf grinned at Puss and connected his sickles together into one menacing two-headed scythe. Then the wolf spun the weapon skillfully and began to attack at an unbelievable speed.

The scythe sliced through Puss's cape and slashed one of his iconic boots. One final slash sent Puss's sword flying, landing a few feet away from him. Unarmed, Puss stood tall as the wolf loomed over him.

"Tsk, tsk," the wolf clicked his tongue at Puss. He charged at Puss again at full throttle. But the wolf underestimated Puss. Even without his cape, a boot, and his sword, Puss wasn't alone anymore. With defiance, Puss unsheathed Kitty's dagger and blocked the scythe. He dove between the wolf's legs and stole back his sword, double-armed with both his own weapon and Kitty's.

The tables had turned. Puss was back in business!

"Pray for mercy," Puss drawled, "*from Puss in Boots*!"

He charged at the wolf with passion, almost dancing across the surface of the star. Puss deftly disarmed the wolf, cutting the mega-scythe into separate halves that clattered down to the ground.

While the fight raged on, Kitty kicked Jack in the face. *POW!* It knocked him right into his magical bottomless bag.

"Aaaah!" Jack's voice echoed as he tumbled into the endless depths.

With Jack now indisposed, Kitty turned her attention on Puss.

Puss was playing the wolf's own game. He kicked a sickle toward the four-legged canine and said, "Pick it up."

The wolf was shocked.

"I know I can never defeat you, lobo. But I will never

stop fighting for this life," Puss said. It was like what Dog had said. This life was the one that mattered.

The wolf took up his blade and stalked toward Puss, and Puss raised his sword. The wolf loomed in close and fixed Puss with a penetrating gaze, but then his expression changed. He growled. He saw something that wasn't there before.

"Oh man. You're ruining this for me," the wolf sighed. "I came here for an arrogant little legend who thought he was immortal, but I don't see him. I only see a gato."

The wolf peered into Puss's eyes for another look, this time just to be sure. And there was no mistaking it. Puss was for *sure* a changed cat—a cat who appreciated life.

The wolf reared back, spun his sickles around, and holstered them in retreat. This was the end of the match.

"Live your life, Puss in Boots. Live it well."

Puss knew they'd meet again one day—when Puss was an old kitten who had lived a full last life. But for now, the wolf turned away. His whistle echoed as he stepped through the curtain of life, gone to stalk new prey whose time had come.

Puss steadied himself, relieved. He'd live to fight another day.

CHAPTER 19

"You know, when you said death was after you, I thought you were being metaphorical," Kitty said. They were still at the wishing star.

Puss handed the map back to Kitty. What he had come here for, he no longer needed. The battle with the wolf had proved that.

"The wish is yours. You deserve someone you can trust," Puss told her, and he meant every word.

Kitty took the map, but she needed it now just as much as Puss did.

"I don't need it," she admitted. "I've got what I've wanted."

There was no magic required.

However, speaking of magic . . . from inside the magical bottomless bag, Jack's voice could be heard. "Oh, magic snacks! Don't mind if I do," he said and chewed as loud as only a deceitful piemaker could. Jack was eating a cookie. With *purpose*.

BELCH! Next came a big old burp right from it, and the bag spewed out a cookie wrapper that said, "Eat Me."

"Ahhh," Jack's voice boomed, satisfied. His voice thundered from inside the bag, very deep and with reverb.

BAM! A giant-sized Jack Horner arose from the tiny bag, like a wicked genie arising from a magic lamp.

"Haha! I was worried for a second that I'd come out naked, but my clothes grew, too. Cool!" Jack said.

Harnessing the power of the "make-him-big" cookie, Jack stretched out one massive hand, snatched up the map, and held it high. It was the size of a playing card in his hands. Puss and Kitty were still holding onto it, too, but Jack knocked Puss and Kitty away with ease. They landed near the edge of the star where the bears were. Expertly, Kitty jammed her sword into the star to keep them from being sucked into the magic. Puss kept his hold tight on Kitty.

"The wish. It's mine!" Jack laughed as the incantation sparkled, and he began to recite it. "I wish I may, I wish I might, have this wish I wish to—"

The wish was almost complete. But then there was a voice.

"Mister Horner!" the voice rung out.

It was *Dog*!

"Please. Please don't make that wish," Dog said.

One of Dog's eyes started twitching. It was getting bigger—bigger . . .

"What are you doing?" Jack shrieked.

Puss and Kitty shrugged at each other. Then Puss stole another look at Dog. He realized something. He figured out what Dog was doing!

"Pleeeee-eeeease!"

Ta-da! Dog had mastered the feline super-cute-eyes! His eyes were big, dewy, and *totally* adorable.

Jack softened. He was no match for the power of Dog's eyes.

"They're such pools of vulnerability. It's so cute—" Jack trailed off. But then he was back. "Did you think that would work on me! Don't you know I'm dead inside?"

"Just buying some time for Team Friendship," Dog said with a grin.

But that moment of distraction was all the Three Bears Crime Family needed. They sprinted toward Jack, with Goldilocks riding Baby in the middle. *VAM!* Baby catapulted Goldilocks forward, launching her toward Jack.

The family had struck a deal with Puss and Kitty, who were perched on Goldilocks's staff! They'd all come to together defeat the would-be tyrant from acquiring too much power.

Goldilocks launched Puss and Kitty into the air. When they reached as high as they were going to go, the cats shared a knowing look. It was now or never. Both cats landed sword-first into Jack's thumbs. (*Yeesh!* It looked like it hurt as Goldilocks landed on Jack's shoulder.)

But for Puss and Kitty, it was all part of the plan.

"The Spanish Splinter!" Puss and Kitty called out at the same time, echoing Puss's fight with the mountain giant that ended his eighth (and penultimate) life.

As Jack yelled in pain, he loosened his grip on the map. Goldilocks dove from Jack's shoulder and caught it before landing safely on the ground with the two cats beside her.

Knowing they couldn't risk Jack wishing for unlimited supplies of magic, and with all their wishes fulfilled, Puss, Kitty, and Goldilocks tore the map to shreds. *SHRRRRP!*

With the map reduced to pitiful pieces, the wishing star began to deteriorate. It bubbled and burst with volcanic stardust.

"What have you done?" Jack called out.

But it was too late. The wishing star began to implode! Goldilocks and the bears raced up a splinter of the collapsing star and landed in a heap on the edge of the star's crater. Then Puss, Kitty, and Dog ran up another vertical splinter of the star, making one giant leap to the cliff. All the outlaws had made it to safety—all except for Jack. Still corrupt with his dreams of power, Jack started sinking into the hot star-lava below, but not before gathering pieces of the map, only one piece missing from the center.

"Ha! Yes! It's mine!" he declared. "Huh?"

Jack looked through the hole in the map, and in the distance saw Ethical Bug riding the back of the flame throwing Phoenix!

"Consider this my resignation, Mister!" Bug called out, waving the final missing piece of the map.

"Curse you, Ethical Bug! I thought we were friends!" The last thing anyone saw—or heard—of Jack Horner was a purple thumb going from a thumbs up to a thumbs down and sinking below the surface to his final demise.

Once it was clear they'd won, the group of seven breathed a sigh of relief.

The star continued imploding, shooting light and power into the skies. As it did, the cosmos shone with silver light, creating millions of shooting stars scattered across the sky, like Puss's original fireworks over Del Mar, only much, much brighter.

No one may have used the wish, but they got what they wanted all the same. And that was what was most important.

EPILOGUE

Goldilocks and the three bears stood and watched the night sky glisten like magnificent fireworks. Baby Bear had tears in his eyes.

"You saved my life, sis. You was gonna make that wish, but you *didn't*, 'cause you wanted to save your family."

"Oi, don't get so blubbery about it. Whose porridge would I eat otherwise?" chimed Goldilocks as she smiled.

"I'm sorry you didn't get your wish, Goldi-love," Mama Bear said. All she wanted was for her cubs to be happy.

"But I did, Mama. I did get my wish," said Goldilocks. "Everything is *just* right."

And so it was. Goldilocks's path had been right from the start. What she wished for—a family—had been in front of her all along.

Meanwhile, Puss and Kitty stared up at the most romantic night sky in history as thousands of falling stars struck across their view.

"I hate to say it," Kitty said to Puss. "But . . . should we make a wish?"

"Kitty, one life, spent with you . . . is all that I could wish for," Puss replied.

The cats smiled at each other. They didn't need a fancy event in Santa Coloma. They had each other—that's all that mattered.

Dog looked up at Puss and Kitty and basked in the happiness, too. But that reminded Puss . . .

"Hey, Perrito, about that name. Let's pick one out for you," Puss said. After all their adventures, it was high time that Dog got some dignity!

"What about Chiquito?" Kitty suggested. It certainly suited Dog well!

"Ah! Chomper! What do you think, perro?"

But Dog wasn't into either of those names. He had an idea all his own.

"You know, if it's the same to you, I think I'll just stick with Perrito, since that's what my friends call me."

For once, Puss didn't bristle at the word "friends."

"Then Perrito it shall be," Kitty said as she smiled at him.

"You know, to be honest, Chomper is pretty good," said Puss.

"Yeah, but no," replied Dog.

"It's okay, we'll keep workshopping it."